LOST TREASURES

BARB GOODWIN
DOUG PENIKAS

SECRETS
OF THE ROYAL
DANISH EGG

This book is dedicated to our family.

The elephants crown the lion's gold
As imperial eagle's crowded case
Lead to the rightful owner's place

The golden afternoon light gently filtered through the large floor-to-ceiling windows illuminating the Fabergé exhibit in the Metropolitan Museum of Art. Eighteen-year-old Rebecca Hunter Lake, Becca, stood in the middle of the room next to a display case and gazed at a Fabergé artifact. Her heart pounded with excitement as she studied the beautifully crafted piece.

On a pedestal underneath protective glass lay an impressive gold, ribbed cigarette case decorated with a lemon-gold double-headed Imperial Eagle. The label read, Made between 1899 and 1904.

A tall, handsome young man with short, dark hair, walked up to the display case, stood right next to her, and stared at the item. A couple of years older than her, the young man wore an expensive brown leather jacket with an asymmetrical zipper, dark gray skinny fit jeans, and black combat boots. He looked like the type of guy who would be on the cover of all the tabloids, but she wouldn't know who he was because she never read any entertainment gossip. He flexed his long fingers by his side and she caught a glimpse of his stunning gold-faced watch with a dark brown leather band. The man glanced at her and gave her a cocky wink, which she found unusually attractive.

He turned back to the display case and studied the Fabergé item.

"Did you know there's a rumor that this cigarette case may contain a secret leading to one of Fabergé's lost eggs?" Becca blabbered, unable to contain her giddiness around the handsome stranger. She realized this was the first time she'd ever talked to someone so cute.

"Really? Where'd you hear that?" he said with a deep voice.

"I'm getting a head start on my thesis for when I start at Columbia University next year. It's about Peter Carl Fabergé and theoretically where one of his seven lost eggs may be located today."

"That seems ambitious. Got any facts to back up your theory?"

"Nothing concrete...yet. I was hoping I'd be allowed to have a curator examine the cigarette case up close for any sign of proof, but the museum shut me down."

"That's expected," the man said. "I would think to get access to any museum piece you'd have to know someone very high up."

She sensed the conversation was coming to an end and wanted to keep chatting. "You know, if I was going to steal it, I'd do it right now, when the sun hits the case and blurs everything around it," Becca joked. "The natural light is perfect to hide any unusual movements. Plus, the guard isn't looking."

The man glanced at her. "You would, would you?" he asked, a wry smile turning up one side of his mouth.

"I would," Becca grinned. "If I knew I could get away with it. Beautiful, isn't it?"

The man's smile widened, but it didn't reach his eyes this time. He barely turned his head to glance at her and he didn't answer her question.

Becca saw the single-minded concentration he directed on the display case. She'd only been talking theoretically. State-of-the-art security cameras were placed strategically around every room of the museum. They would easily catch a misguided thief's attempt to steal a priceless item.

She glanced around the empty room. The male guard at the far corner was still looking away.

"How would you steal it?" she asked. "In theory."

He pulled out his smartphone.

"Like this."

He pressed an app with his thumb and the cigarette display case immediately popped open a fraction of an inch. Startled, Becca looked at the security cameras and noticed the green light was out on all of them.

In less than five seconds, the man lifted the cigarette case out and replaced it with an exact duplicate. Becca knew there were pressure sensors that would set off alarms when a change occurred, but to her surprise, no alarms went off. The man slipped the cigarette case into his inside jacket pocket, closed the display case, and pressed the app on his phone one more time. Becca glanced back at the security cameras and saw the green lights were active once again.

The thief looked at Becca and gave her a wide, charming smile. He patted his jacket pocket and said, "Ciao, Beautiful," then turned to leave.

"You...you just stole that." Becca's mind raced, as she comprehended what just happened. "Wait. Stop. THIEF!" she shouted and pointed at the man.

"Not cool," the thief muttered.

"Hey! What's going on here?" shouted the guard from the other side of the room.

"I just saw that guy steal the cigarette case!" Becca said.

"What?" the man said with fake innocence. "I was just looking."

The guard spoke into his walkie-talkie. "Possible theft in the Fabergé room. Lockdown the museum. Call the police."

"This is ridiculous," the man said. "She's crazy."

The guard cautiously approached the man. "Sir, I need you to empty your pockets."

Two more guards hurried into the room and blocked the exit.

"It's in his inside left jacket pocket," Becca added.

"I need you to keep your hands in sight," the guard said. "You too, lady."

"I didn't do anything," Becca told the guard. "I swear."

Alarms rang throughout the building. A gate slid down from the ceiling, trapping everyone in the Fabergé exhibit.

"This is all a big misunderstanding," the thief said, still playing the innocent act as he backed away from the guards and closer to Becca.

"Keep your hands where we can see them. We're going to search both of you," the first guard said.

In a quick move, the thief grabbed Becca and pulled her into his arms. He whipped out a knife and held it to her neck. Her heart raced with fear. They'd just been flirting and now she was his hostage.

The three guards drew their weapons.

"Open the gate," the thief demanded in a calm, threatening tone.

Becca forced herself to think rationally amidst the chaos. The knife blade was razor-sharp and must have been made of ceramic material. The blade wasn't cold against her neck and she knew the thief couldn't have brought a metal knife into the museum. It wouldn't have gotten through the metal detectors.

The guard's walkie-talkie squawked. "This is the police. We're coming in."

The thief kept Becca close, using her as a human shield. She watched the gate rise and the room dedicated to Fabergé's priceless artifacts filled with armed police officers who surrounded Becca and the thief.

Dizzy from being yanked around, fear feeding her adrenaline, Becca pulled on the man's arm to keep the knife from touching her neck. Using all her strength, she twisted away as she jerked the knife from his hand. It fell to the floor and shattered into pieces.

She was free.

The police rushed the thief and pinned him to the ground. Becca watched as they roughly put his hands behind his back, cuffed him, and read him his rights. Two officers lifted the thief to his feet and held him still while a third patted him down.

"No weapons. The only thing on him was this," one officer said.

Becca watched the officer hand the real cigarette case to his superior. The superior officer walked over to her and asked, "Is this the item you saw that man take?"

"Yes," she replied, trying to control her emotions. "I saw him put a fake in the display case when he took the real one out of it."

"Let's have the curator inspect the cigarette case that's on display right now," the officer told the head security guard.

"He's on his way," the guard replied.

A few minutes later the curator, a tall, thin man in his sixties arrived and went straight to the police officer in charge. Becca didn't talk with the man, but his erect posture and bland expression gave her the impression of a stuffy, middle-aged man.

The officer handed the curator the real cigarette case, which he inspected thoroughly. Then the curator opened the display case to inspect the fake. He turned them both over, felt the gold ribs on the outside of each, glanced inside the cases, and did another complete inspection to differentiate the two. He held up his left hand and with a nod of his head he said, "This is the real one."

The curator opened the display case and returned the real cigarette case to its proper place on display for all to see. He handed the fake to the officer in charge. "Get rid of this monstrosity."

Becca saw the thief watching the curator with narrowed eyes. As two police officers escorted him past her, the thief leaned forward, putting his face in Becca's. His eyes glared with rage and frightened her.

"I'm going to find you," he growled. "You have no idea what you're getting into."

The police officers struggled to pull the thief away from Becca. The thief rammed his body into the superior officer, who tried to hold onto Becca to keep from falling but wasn't successful. The officer lost his grip on the fake cigarette case and fell to the floor.

The force of the falling officer caused Becca to lose her balance. She tripped into the back of the curator's legs, causing them to buckle under him. In the process, the curator kicked the whole display case over and the top popped open. The real cigarette case fell out.

As everyone fell to the floor, the real case slid near Becca. She saw the fake case as it fell out of the officer's hand and watched it slide next to the real case.

The thief made a run for it.

The officers scrambled to their feet to aid the museum security guards as they tackled the thief and pinned him to the floor.

Becca noticed no one was looking at the cigarette cases. Acting on impulse, she switched the two cases on the floor.

When the curator got up, he grabbed the fake cigarette case off the floor. The curator didn't pay attention to the case he'd just grabbed, as he appeared to be more concerned about his flustered appearance in front of all the police officers. She watched him fix his shirt, his tie, and his hair as others righted the overturned display case.

Too preoccupied with his appearance, the curator quickly placed the fake in the display case. He closed and locked the top. "The real case is back where it belongs." He glanced around. "Are we done here?"

The officer in charge returned to Becca and the curator after securing the thief. He picked up the cigarette case from the floor, not knowing he now held the real one. "If all is in order for you, we can take care of the rest."

The curator pointed to the thief. "I never want to see him in my museum again." He stormed off in a tizzy.

"Here," the officer in charge said to Becca, holding out the real cigarette case. "You helped us catch our perp. Seems a waste to throw a nice knock-off away. Keep it as a reminder for being a good citizen."

Becca couldn't believe it. It was so simple. The distraction of the thief mixed with the curator's self-absorbed attitude had masked the deception. Becca knew she should do the right thing, wanted to do the right thing, but to her own surprise, she took the real cigarette case from the officer and simply replied, "Thank you. Just doing what I can."

She put the case in her pocket and saw the thief glaring at her. She knew he was the only one in the entire room who knew the truth.

Becca now had the real cigarette case and all she had to do was walk out the front door of the museum.

2

Hours later, Becca exited the apartment bathroom wearing a robe and a towel around her head. She lived with her mother in a two-bedroom apartment, but her mother was visiting friends for a few days. She double-checked the front door, making certain it was securely locked. She had left the shades open so she could see the lights of New York City when she'd left earlier, but decided to close the shades, now paranoid by the feeling that someone might be watching her from afar. The feeling of constantly looking over her shoulder overwhelmed her since she had committed a crime for the first time in her life. What was even worse, she was excited she had succeeded.

She sat down at the dining room table and pulled the Fabergé cigarette case from her bathrobe pocket to study it. Her hands shook as she turned the case over, rubbed the back, and marveled that she held something Peter Carl Fabergé himself had made.

Becca turned the case to the front and carefully lifted the lid. There was nothing inside. She re-examined it, studied the weight of it, and traced the ornamental design. She ran her fingers along the inside of the case and found a tiny latch. *Click*. A false bottom opened and inside was a fragile, folded rough-textured piece of paper.

Her heart pounded as she delicately opened the paper, careful not to rip it. Becca gasped with excitement as she read,

37Prepar°er6178Ecastelet557N5gui17chet°

Her excitement crashed into disappointment. "What does this mean?" she muttered.

She couldn't believe it. After constant rejections from the museum's curator to examine the case up close, she finally had closure in knowing she'd been correct. Something had been inside, but it didn't make any sense. It was pure gibberish.

A knock thudded on the door, followed by a voice. "Delivery."

"Thank God." Becca's stomach grumbled. She hadn't eaten for hours. She quickly placed the fragile paper back in the secret compartment of the cigarette case, shoved it under one of the couch cushions, then opened the door revealing an angry delivery man. After seconds of wondering why the man was angry with her, she realized he wasn't a delivery person at all; he was the thief from the museum.

The thief shoved into her room before she could slam the door in his face.

Becca's heart pounded with fear.

He smiled. "Found you." He closed and locked the door behind him then stepped closer to her. "All it took was a glance at the paperwork the arresting officer left carelessly on his desk and I knew where to come, Rebecca Hunter Lake."

She backed away and bumped into the coffee table. "Get the hell away from me!" Becca grabbed her cell phone and dialed 911.

"That won't work right now." He glared.

Becca's phone had no signal. She hurried to the landline phone and picked it up. The line was dead.

The thief held up his smartphone. "Jamming app. No phone will work within a one-hundred-yard radius while it's activated."

Realizing she was trapped, she hung up the phone and decided to stall as she planned her escape. "What do you want?"

"I saw what you did at the museum. Pretty smooth. Using distraction as your ally to make a simple lift. You've got skills, but you've become a royal pain in my ass today and I want the case back."

"No."

The thief squeezed his fists, gritted his teeth, and moved closer to her. She kept a good distance between them.

"Look, you seem like a nice girl. Annoying, but nice. I meant what I said earlier. You really have no idea what you're getting yourself into. So just hand over the piece and I'll be on my way."

"Why do you want it?"

"I won't tell you that. The less you know the better. For your own sake. Now hand it over."

"It's not here," she lied, hoping to get him to leave. "I returned it to the museum anonymously."

The thief ignored her and searched the desk drawers and the couch cushions. He pulled up the cushion and found the case, holding it up for display as he turned and smiled. "You need to work on your lying skills." Becca hoped to make a run for it, but the thief would be between her and the front door before she could get there.

She sucked in a breath. Was the thief armed? Would he hurt her? "You have what you want. Just go." She watched the man for aggressive behavior. He showed none now that he had the cigarette case. It didn't matter to her who had the case. Becca had seen the text inscribed on the old paper and thanks to her God-given gift of a photographic memory, her mind had already memorized it.

In a way, the thief was doing her a favor by taking the case off her hands. She wouldn't have to worry about the police finding it in her possession. All that needed to be done was to have him leave or to get away from him.

The thief opened the door then stopped and faced her in the doorway. "I watched you cleverly take the case from the museum at the perfect time when no one else would notice, and now you're not even putting up a fight to keep it…"

Becca saw the realization on his face.

"You figured it out already, didn't you?"

Becca's silence betrayed her. The thief closed and locked the door behind him "What did you find?"

Becca stayed silent.

"I don't have time to fool around with you," the thief said, "as much as I'd like to."

She couldn't believe he was hitting on her now. Only a few hours ago he held her at knifepoint. "Who are you?"

"Reed Alexander Carter. You can call me RC."

Are you kidding me? Of all the things to happen to her today, one of the most notorious, womanizing, Forbes top-thirty-under-thirty trust fund babies with a secret propensity for thievery, was standing in her apartment. She had heard his name from her good-for-nothing father. Reed Alexander Carter was from a famous family who used their riches to hunt for lost treasures. A hobby that had split her own family apart. She had never seen a photo of RC before because that kind of tabloid nonsense didn't hold her attention. If it wasn't history, she wasn't interested.

"What douche has three first names?" was all she could say as her mind raced a hundred miles a minute.

RC grinned as he moved away from the door and closer to Becca. She backed away from him.

"I need you to answer me honestly. Do you know what's inside the case?"

"No." She stood her ground and hoped he'd believe her.

"Don't lie to me. Your life depends on your honesty."

She caught a sense of protectiveness in his tone, which confused her even more. "Why would I tell you anything when you keep threatening me? You have the case. Leave me alone."

"I can't," he said frustrated. He made his way past her to the window and cautiously peered through the crack between the shades. "Now they'll hunt you everywhere you go."

Becca felt a cold chill creep up her spine. "Who?"

RC turned off the jamming app and made a call. "I've got a baby who needs a nest." He hung up the phone.

"What are you talking about? Who was that? I thought you were the one after me." She didn't like how his words frightened her. "Just go."

"Sweetheart, you wish I was the only one after you."

His phone buzzed. He answered, looking out the window again staying off to the side. "Meet in the parking lot around the back in five." RC hung up his phone and headed toward the front door. "Come on, we're leaving. Change into something fast. You'll be safe with—"

Becca smashed RC in the head with a table lamp, knocking him out cold on the floor.

3

"This is all I have on me, Barry. I knocked him out, threw on my clothes, grabbed my cell phone wallet, and got the hell out of there. The dude is creepy." Becca brought Barry, her best friend since they were eight years old, up to speed over breakfast at his favorite coffee shop the next morning.

"I'm still trying to get over the fact that you left Reed Alexander Carter unconscious in your apartment. If only the paparazzi were there. You'd be famous."

"I'm serious, Barry."

"I know. I just wanted to lighten the mood."

"I'm telling you, we were right. There was a clue in the cigarette case. I just don't know what it means."

You've had a crazy twenty-four hours. What did he mean by, "You wish I was the only one after you?"

"I don't know and I didn't want to stay to find out."

"Let me see what was inside the case."

"I need a pen."

Barry got one out of his backpack and handed it to her. She quickly scribbled out the letters, numbers, and symbols on a paper napkin then pushed it toward him.

"I wish I had your memory."

Barry's envy was no secret to her. He loved watching her look at random textbooks and instantly be able to reproduce paragraphs accurately. It was one of his favorite games to play with her and he'd always used her to win other classmates' lunch money in high school.

Barry took a sip of coffee and studied the script.

"I looked up the words on my way over here," Becca said. "Preparer comes from the Latin verb parere which means to try to get. Guichet is a French word and it means a grating, a hatch, or a small opening in a wall, and castelet is French for a small castle. But none of the words make any sense together, and I have no idea how the numbers and symbols fit in with the puzzle."

"It doesn't look like any anagram that I'm familiar with. Let me run it through Josephine to see what she comes up with."

"I still can't believe you named your computer." Becca cracked up at how giddy Barry looked as he pulled out his laptop from his backpack and booted it up. He didn't respond to her. His laser focus always kicked in when he was excited about something. It was one of the many things Becca enjoyed about Barry. He was as smart as she was, but without her photographic memory. Plus, his analytical mind worked better when he was figuring out a problem or puzzle. If she needed something researched beyond the norm, extracted from a computer, deciphered, or whatever...she called Barry.

She took a bite of her scrambled eggs. The waiter refilled their cups with steaming coffee.

"Thank you," Becca said with a sigh. She wasn't a great morning person, and coffee always helped keep her alert.

"It's not an Enigma code or Caesar Shift cipher," Barry said, not looking away from the screen. He typed some more.

"Latin and French," Becca mumbled, "prepare a grating or hatch in a wall in a castle? What castle?"

Barry straightened. "What did you say?"

Before she could reply, RC strode up to the table, grabbed a chair from the empty table next to them, placed it between her and Barry, turned it around, and casually leaned his arms across the back, looking at her.

"Hi, there," he said, ignoring Barry's existence.

Becca tensed with fear as she saw the calm, cold stare in RC's eyes. "How...did you find me?" Her chest tightened and she felt herself taking small, shallow breaths. She saw Barry cover the napkin with his laptop and to her relief, RC didn't seem to notice.

"You know what?" RC began as he grabbed a piece of bacon off Becca's plate and took a bite. "I have a massive headache. You've become a royal pain in my ass, girl."

Two men dressed in dark suits with white shirts and dark sunglasses stopped at their table between Becca and RC. Becca immediately knew something was wrong by the way they carried themselves and how they towered over them like mercenaries about to torture their captives. They looked government, but something was off.

"You three," one of the men said with a very intense baritone voice, "You need to come with us. Now."

The undertone of his words gave them no choice. Becca looked at RC, expecting them to be his bodyguards, but the slight shake of his head and the look on his face confirmed that RC had never seen these men before.

Becca saw the bulge of the firearms they carried under their suit coats. She could tell both men were right-handed by the fact that their concealed weapons were on their right side. If she wanted to get away, she'd maybe have half a second to do so before they drew their guns on them.

She glanced at Barry's full cup of coffee, then at RC. His eyes drifted to the same cup and without speaking a word she knew he understood what she planned to do. With no intent to comply, she took a sip of her coffee then asked, "What's this about?" Becca didn't have the cigarette case on her anymore so she knew she was in the clear, but these two men didn't look like they were from the museum. "Who are you? FBI? Secret Service? NSA?"

Ignoring her questions, the leader of the two men grabbed Becca's left arm and pulled her out of her chair. With her right hand, Becca threw her coffee into the leader's face, forcing him to let go. At the same time, RC grabbed Barry's coffee and threw it into the other man's face.

Both men hollered in pain as the scalding coffee burned their skin. They each grabbed a glass of ice water off the table and tossed it onto their faces to quell the stinging.

RC grabbed Becca's hand and they raced toward the kitchen. Barry grabbed his laptop, its case, and hurried after them.

The two men gave chase.

RC led Becca and Barry through the kitchen, out the back door, and up a side street, through a t-shirt shop, out its back door, and down another street.

Becca wondered if he knew where he was going. Stumbling to keep up, she was rapidly running out of breath. "Hold up. I need to stop." She leaned against a building wall.

"You need to work out more," RC said.

"Who were those guys?" Barry looked back to make sure they weren't followed.

"The ones I warned her about last night," RC said.

"You're blaming me?" she gasped between deep breaths.

"Yeah. If you hadn't clocked me, this wouldn't be happening." His tone annoyed her but Becca knew he was right.

"We need to keep moving. Pace your breathing." RC dragged her into a coffee shop two doors down, where they stood in a corner out of sight. Becca's breathing slowly returned to normal while RC watched out the windows. Patrons of the shop looked at them curiously, but no one said anything.

"By the way, I do work out," Becca corrected, "I just don't run." She leaned her head against a wall and looked longingly at a cup of iced coffee.

"Do you think we lost them?" Barry asked, looking out another window, worried.

Becca watched RC glance around the coffee shop. He stopped when he saw something in the corner on the ceiling. Becca followed his gaze and noticed a security camera watching them.

Becca put two and two together. "You don't think they…"

"We need to go right now!" RC said.

"What is that?" Barry asked with fear.

Becca and RC both looked out the window and saw a black SUV heading straight for them.

"Move!" RC pulled Becca out of the way and covered her with his body as they both dove to the checkered floor. Barry jumped in the opposite direction.

Crash!

The SUV blasted through the coffee shop entrance, shattering the windows. Glass flew across the room, people screamed and jumped out of the way of the vehicle. Tables were smashed, shelves were destroyed, and the pastry display case was demolished.

Dazed, Becca looked beneath the SUV and saw Barry crawling on the other side of the shop toward the damaged entrance. Thank God he was alive.

"Are you okay?" RC asked as he helped her to her feet. "Can you run?"

"I think…think so." Becca watched the driver's side door open and the man in the suit got out of the vehicle with his silenced weapon drawn.

"Come on." RC hustled her to the back entrance of the shop, out the door, and into an alley.

Becca found her bearings and was able to run without RC's aid.

The two men ran after them and fired two shots at Becca and RC. The bullets hit the stone walls, barely missing them as they turned the corner.

Becca followed RC down the stairs into a subway station. He

fished in his pockets, pulled out two tickets, and shoved one into Becca's hand.

Luckily, the train was already boarding as Becca and RC jumped through the doors just as they began to shut. They were the last to get on before the doors closed.

As the train pulled away from the station, Becca looked out the window and saw the two pursuers enter through the turnstiles and realize they couldn't keep up. Becca leaned against the pole and heaved a sigh of relief, knowing she and RC had escaped.

"They'll find us," RC said, dashing her hopes.

His alertness annoyed her. His eyes moved over everyone on the train. Plus, they were being stared at. Their clothes were dusty and ripped, they had spots of blood on them from the broken glass at the coffee shop.

"They shot at us." Becca couldn't believe it. "Why would they shoot at us?"

"Just breathe," RC said with a calm, quiet tone. "The adrenaline will wear off in a few minutes."

"I don't want any part of this. It's not worth being shot at."

"It's too late now," RC said. "They know about you and as you saw, they will not stop until they get what they want. In their eyes, you are enemy number one."

Fear encapsulated her as she replayed in her mind how the two men could have found them. "They hacked the security feed at the coffee shop, didn't they? That's how they knew where we were."

He nodded. "And most likely every camera from your apartment to the coffee shop."

"Who has that kind of access? They're not government. I can't believe they're the government." She thought of seeing Barry on the ground crawling to safety and prayed he got away. She needed to text him. Her thoughts then shifted to her own safety, realizing how dangerous her situation had become. "Give the case to them. I never wanted this. They could have killed Barry, or us!"

"Keep your voice down." RC leaned close to Becca and in a harsh whisper said, "We don't want to draw any more attention. They could be on this train right now."

"Who are they? How do you know about them?"

"All you need to know right now is that I'm the one who will keep you alive." He looked right into her eyes. She knew he was serious and for some reason, she believed him. "But you have to trust me…and no more lamps on the back of my head."

He reached toward her and removed a shard of crushed glass from her hair. She realized she hadn't jumped at his touch, and for some odd reason, much like how they first met at the museum, she felt oddly safe in his presence.

"Give me your phone." He held out his hand.

Becca saw a strangely shaped flesh-colored scar that was reminiscent of the claw of a bird on the inside of his right wrist. She wondered what could have caused such a strange injury.

Hesitant at first, she took her phone out of her pocket and handed it to him. She watched him activate an app on his phone and a light scanned hers.

Surprisingly, no one on the train noticed or seemed to care.

"They can hack into the security feed on any camera in the city. Phones are no different." RC finished scanning her phone and put his own back in his pocket. "Mine's encrypted. We need to get you off the grid." The train stopped at the next station. "Wait here."

RC ran off and tossed her phone into the train on the track next to them, then hurried back onto their train. They watched the other train leave the station going in the opposite direction their train would take them. "That should buy us a few hours."

Thousands of questions raced through Becca's mind but all she could ask was, "Where are we going?"

"To safety," he replied simply.

She really hated the clouds of mystery that surrounded Reed Alexander Carter and his cryptic responses, but if there was one thing that today proved, whatever she was involved in, she was in way over her head.

4

"This is safety?" Becca asked as she gazed at the three-story estate prominently lit by the afternoon light. They stood at an imposing iron gate with a high-tech video and security system displayed to deter the unworthy.

RC put his eye up to a retinal scanner and the gate swung open.

"Welcome to my home." He smiled.

The hair on Becca's arms stood up. She'd never seen a home that big. Except on reality TV.

They walked up a beautifully landscaped brick path that wound between old oak trees. Perfectly green lawns sloped away from a path decorated with seasonal flowers. A scent of roses filled the air as Becca stared at the gray stone exterior and a gray steepled roof that was partially covered by climbing ivy. Large bushes leaned against the front wall and a high patio cover shaded a very large entrance. She couldn't help but wonder if there was a west wing with an enchanted rose losing its petals being guarded by a monster somewhere inside.

As soon as Becca and RC stepped onto the massive front porch, the double oak doors with beautifully crafted gold doorknockers opened inward revealing a tuxedoed butler.

"Shall I prepare a guest room or will the young lady be staying in yours?" the butler asked RC.

Becca glanced at RC, embarrassed.

"I'd rather the dog stayed with me, Winston," RC replied dryly.

Becca gave RC a long, slow glare.

"We don't have a dog, sir." Winston gave Becca a comforting smile.

"Exactly." RC smiled at Becca's annoyance with him. "Please have some iced tea brought to the living room."

"How do you like it, Miss?"

"Uh—is it okay if I have a Diet Coke instead?"

"Certainly, Miss," Winston replied.

She couldn't stand being called Miss. "Just Becca, please."

"Pleasure to have you with us, Becca." Winston nodded and left to get the beverages.

Becca followed RC into the living room and gawked at its beauty and enormity. Large picture windows overlooked the front lawn and entryway. A grouping of sofas and chairs was arranged around a double-sided fireplace open to a family room on the other side. A stunning fresh flower arrangement graced the large, square, glass coffee table, emitting a fresh, sweet aroma. What looked like original artwork lined the walls, with individual lights perched over each. It was more like a museum, not a home.

"Make yourself comfortable," RC said dismissively.

She didn't think that would be possible. Becca sat on one of the two white couches in the room. Even though she'd never admit it to RC, the couch was extremely comfortable, especially after the day she'd had.

Winston entered and put a tray with two frosty glasses, a pitcher of iced tea, cream, and brown sugar, as well as Becca's Diet Coke, on the coffee table.

"Would you like me to pour?"

"No, thank you, Winston. We'll be fine."

The butler left and silence filled the room. RC poured iced tea into his glass, added brown sugar, and reached for Becca's Diet Coke can. Becca deliberately grabbed the can before he could, opened it, and drank straight from it. RC raised one eyebrow as he stirred his iced tea. They stared at each other for a long moment with only the sound of RC's stirrer clinking in his chilled glass.

As Becca sipped her Diet Coke, a woman entered the room.

"Reed Alexander, give your mother a hug."

RC winced.

Mrs. Carter wore a white skirt with a matching double-breasted, three-quarter length sleeved blazer, medium black heels, and three strands of evenly matched pitch-black pearls around her neck. Her hair was perfectly styled in a French twist, and her makeup was understated but elegant. Becca felt the temperature drop one hundred degrees with Mrs. Carter's presence.

She wasn't entirely surprised to hear that RC's mother didn't use his nickname. There was no doubt she was queen of the castle and all who opposed her would lose their heads, even her own son.

RC walked stiffly up to her and put his arms loosely around her shoulders. She gave him an air kiss on either cheek. "What have you been up to, dear?" Mrs. Carter sized Becca up. "And who is your lovely…guest?"

Becca had never felt so judged in her life. She'd survived her high school classmates, but this was on a whole other level.

"You must've awakened on the right side of the bed this morning to notice someone else in this house besides yourself. Good for you, Mother."

Becca was shocked to see that Mrs. Carter didn't reply with the typical motherly authoritative response to RC's rudeness. Instead, she brushed it off as if his behavior was normal. She couldn't help but wonder what kind of home RC had been raised in. She almost felt sorry for him, millions, and all.

"Mother, this is Becca. We met yesterday. She's helping me with a case."

"Will...Becca be staying for dinner?"

"No—" Becca tried to answer.

"Yes, she will. We still have work to do," RC interrupted.

The way RC and his mother had been talking, as if she wasn't in the room, made Becca feel invisible. She didn't know what RC was planning and she didn't want to stick around to find out, especially with his mother there. She could see Mrs. Carter wasn't pleased.

"Did she bring anything else to wear for dinner?" Mrs. Carter struggled to ask the question, obviously irritated at the sight of Becca's current appearance.

Becca looked at her own wardrobe, feeling very self-conscious. "Well, I—"

RC interrupted again. "Have Winston set four plates for dinner, Mother." His undertone clearly showed he didn't want to discuss anything more about Becca.

"She'll be seated next to you, across from me."

The distasteful tone of Mrs. Carter's voice grated on Becca's soul. She rapidly lost patience with Mrs. Carter's better-than-thou attitude toward her and RC constantly answering for her.

"I look forward to seeing you both at dinner," Mrs. Carter said, meaning the exact opposite, as she exited the living room.

"Well, that certainly explains a lot," Becca said. "Did hell freeze over?"

"Pretty much," RC replied.

Becca could tell RC didn't want to go into any details about his relationship with his mother, and honestly, she didn't want him to. She just wanted to get out of here. She walked to the front door and opened it. From behind her, RC reached over her shoulder and slammed the door shut.

"Where do you think you're going?"

"I want to go home."

"Need I remind you there are men chasing you who want to kill you?"

For a brief moment, the overly polite conversation between RC and his mother had made Becca forget the danger of her situation. She was trapped.

"I'd rather be chased by them instead of stuck here with your mom."

RC chuckled. "I know what you mean. At least here you're protected from them."

She hated knowing he was right. Plus, she hated the snarky smile on his face, confirming he knew he was right.

Leaning over her, RC said in a steely voice, "I think you ought to reconsider your invitation to dinner."

She had a difficult time processing that she had to spend more time with these pretentious people. Pasting a pleasant smile on her face was not her strong suit. Becca straightened and squared her shoulders. "Considering the circumstances, I'll be happy to accept your mother's invitation to dinner," she said mimicking his mother in an upper-class tone of voice. Then returning to her own voice, "Is there somewhere I can wash my face?"

The tension in RC's face lessened. It changed his look from a harsh man into a kinder, more approachable version, but not by much.

He motioned to a beautiful oak stairway and said, "Bathroom is past the stairway on your left."

Becca gave RC a weak smile and walked into the bathroom. Once she shut the door behind her, she sagged against it for long moments. Then she stepped to the pedestal sink and washed the dirt off her hands, arms, and face. Black streaks of filthy water drained down the sink basin. She pulled broken shards of glass out of her hair and tossed them in the trash, wishing she'd had her purse with her where she always kept a small hairbrush. She used the just-for-display hand towel, not caring, and rehung it. Then she let out a frustrated exhale. It was time to face the Carter family.

With renewed determination, Becca stared into the mirror. "You can do this. It's only one dinner." Taking a deep breath, she raised her head, squared her shoulders, and opened the door to the unknown.

5

Within the first five minutes of sitting at the Carter family table, Becca felt an intense throbbing in the middle of her forehead every time RC's mother spoke. She went on and on about what charity did what and which famous actor, politician, or well-off businessman was in attendance. That Mrs. Carter didn't realize or, worse, didn't care about what anyone else had done during their day spoke louder than any conversation could. She was all about status and it sickened Becca to the bone.

At the head of the table sat RC's father, Mason Carter, a man in his mid-forties, with thick dark hair, a strong, square face, and an intense authoritative presence. Even though he was more than twenty years older than her and quite menacing, he was devilishly attractive, and surprisingly more down to earth than his wife. Becca had no doubt where RC got his looks.

"Becca, I assume it's short for Rebecca," Mason said with a deep voice once Mrs. Carter finished blabbering.

"This is the first time RC's brought a girl back home. Tell us about yourself."

His gentle probing didn't go unnoticed. But what he was probing for was unclear.

Becca hesitated before she answered. "I just graduated high school and plan to take a year off to travel to Europe. I've always wanted to travel."

Mason's curious look of interest gave Becca an uneasy feeling.

"That's a risky gamble," Mason said. "Taking a year off often leads to not going to college at all."

"Oh, that won't happen to me." Becca shook her head. "I'm definitely going." Winston placed another can of Diet Coke next to her plate while she continued. "I want a degree in metallurgy with a secondary degree in mechanical engineering and a third in gemology."

RC laughed at the stunned look on his parent's faces. "Well, Becca, I think you're the first person to ever render my parents speechless." RC took a bite of his blue cheese wedge salad with unexpected satisfaction.

"What a coincidence. Sherylynn has three degrees from Wellesley. Isn't that right, dear?" said Mason.

"But not in such tiresome subjects." Mrs. Carter voiced her negative opinion. "Why those fields?" she asked.

"Look at her," Mason chimed in. "Given the current state of her, she clearly has a taste for adventure."

Becca cringed, feeling so out of place wearing her ripped t-shirt and jeans. She had cleaned her face and arms, but the rest of her clothing was stained and in disarray from her escape from the men chasing her. She hated the fact that there was nothing she could do about it.

"I like a girl who's willing to get her hands dirty," RC added.

"No proper lady would ever go out in public looking like your friend," Mrs. Carter chided.

"I didn't." Becca's blood boiled. "I was chased by men with guns who shot at me. We barely escaped. You try to keep your fancy clothes clean when men are firing guns at you."

A dead silence filled the room. Becca wasn't embarrassed. She'd had it with Mrs. Carter belittling her appearance and felt satisfaction at Mrs. Carter's quietness.

"It's a good thing you brought Ms. Lake here," Mason said to RC as he took a bite of his pork medallions.

Becca couldn't believe it. She'd never mentioned her last name to anyone but could tell that Mason, a stranger, knew everything about her.

"How do you know my last name?"

"I have a very extensive security system that does a background check on all my guests," Mason said casually. "Your full name is Rebecca Hunter Lake. You speak English, Russian, German, and Danish fluently, and read some Latin. You love science and math and hope to put those skills to good use when you complete college.

"Your father is Edward Lake, who makes his money acquiring rare artifacts all over the world. Your mother, Vivian Hunter Lake, is a stay-at-home mom who went to Ohio State and dropped out in her second year. You are an only child, eighteen years of age, and met my son at the Metropolitan Museum of Art yesterday afternoon at the Fabergé exhibit. Now you find yourself here and whether you know it or not, you need my help."

Becca's fork clattered on the plate. "I've suddenly lost my appetite." She'd had enough of RC's parents, and felt like the only one in the room who didn't know what was going on. It was time for answers. "Who are you?" she asked more forcefully than intended, "And more importantly, who are the men hunting me?"

"Winston, we'll have coffee in my office," Mason said, not answering Becca's question.

Winston nodded and immediately left the dining room.

"Sherylynn," Mason faced his wife, who kept her disapproving eyes on Becca. "Ms. Lake, RC, and I have business to discuss."

With deference, Mrs. Carter replied, "Yes, of course, dear." She elegantly stood from her chair and exited the room. Becca couldn't miss the disgusted look Mrs. Carter threw in her direction before the door closed behind her. The lack of protest from Mrs. Carter in response to Mason's request showed Becca a strange sense of hierarchy in the household. Mason was boss, no matter how much Mrs. Carter was in control. It was clear his word was law, and she was either slave to or in agreement with their arrangement.

Mason Carter's office was filled with handcrafted dark cherry wood furniture, a massive customized bookshelf that held brick-thick books that looked hundreds of years old and were probably all first editions. Two wingback leather chairs sat across from a large executive desk. Three cups of steaming coffee had been placed on the desk.

Mason sat in his high-backed swivel chair that appeared more like a throne in Becca's eyes, and poured cream into his coffee before sipping.

Mason's demeanor radiated strictly business. "Tell me why you were at the museum in the first place," he said calmly.

"I thought you knew everything about me." Becca could tell RC found humor in her frankness with his parents.

The way Mason looked at her with such a commanding presence made her realize if she wanted to play games, she would lose. "My wife might not be the most polite person in the world, Ms. Lake, but believe me when I say I have no tolerance for your attitude. Now start from the beginning."

Becca had to clear her throat. "I decided to start my thesis for college in my senior year of high school. I chose to write about Fabergé's missing eggs. I figured a thesis based on existing facts leading to where they might be hidden today would be a decent subject. I like historical mysteries." She felt a little embarrassed about her chosen passion, knowing it wasn't normal, plus RC's surprised reaction confirmed it. "During my research I discovered something."

"Fabergé, with all his glitzy and glittery eggs, must have liked bling," RC said sarcastically. "His eggs are detailed and ornate. He was way ahead of his time. You could say he liked to bedazzle things. Imagine what he'd do to an iPhone." Mason raised a hand for RC to shut up and waited for Becca to continue.

"I contacted the Fabergé Museum in St. Petersburg to get any information they had on the last-known locations of the seven lost eggs. Aleksi Bogatir, a Fabergé historian who's a descendant of one of Peter Carl Fabergé's apprentices, contacted me from Moscow, where he lived. For months we emailed back and forth, even had a few phone calls, cross-referencing any and all rumored locations with their records to find if there were any correlations between the two. I spent days, if not weeks, following leads until a dead end presented itself, which became the norm. I contacted other employees of Fabergé about their grandparents and great grandparents to find more clues they might have been told from their childhood that could lead to a new path to follow."

"You must be a very resourceful girl," Mason said, seeming impressed by her ambition.

"Aleksi was gracious in answering all my questions about Fabergé's craft, his passion for perfection, and even how he inspired his employees to add that passion to their everyday lives."

"Get to the part about the museum," RC said.

Becca shot him an annoyed glance and then skipped ahead in her story. "Yesterday morning I had an email from Aleksi time-stamped at 3:32 a.m., New York time. The subject line read I think I'm being followed. It was a very strange email."

"Do you still have it?" Mason asked.

Becca shook her head no.

"I ditched her phone, to make sure she wasn't being tracked before I brought her here," RC explained.

Mason flipped a switch somewhere behind his desk and a hologram of a woman hovered in the middle of his office. "DIANA, access email for Rebecca Hunter Lake."

DIANA's electronic female voice responded, *Searching.*

"DIANA?" Becca asked.

"D.I.A.N.A.," Mason explained. "Stands for Data Interactive Algorithmic Network Application."

Becca gasped as all her emails appeared in the middle of the room for all to see. "What about my password?"

"Decryption software," Mason answered.

"What's Disco Dance Puppy?" RC asked.

Becca ignored RC's question and did her best to hide her embarrassment. It was a cute video that always put her in a good mood, but she'd never admit that to RC, less ammunition for his prying mind.

"Access 'I think I'm being followed'," Mason said.

The email flickered from all the others and jumped to the front of the hologram.

Opening, 'I think I'm being followed' from aleksib@houseoffab.com.

The entire email opened and the hologram read the message out loud in Aleksi Bogatir's voice. Hearing her contact's voice as if he was in the room freaked Becca out.

Dear Becca, I don't mean to alarm you, but I think I'm being followed. I regret to say my father passed away three days ago of natural causes. In his final moments, he confessed what he called a family secret to me. In my humble opinion, it doesn't mean anything, because my father was on multiple medications and not always coherent. He said the following:

The elephants crown the lion's gold, as imperial eagle's clouded case, lead to the rightful owner's place.

When I mentioned this to my fellow colleagues at work, they didn't know what it meant. On my bike ride home that night a car appeared to be following me. That same vehicle showed up the next morning when I went to work. It was across the street from where I get lunch, and again that evening as I left to go home. This all began after I told my colleagues about my father's message, and I couldn't help but be reminded of our past emails about the history surrounding the missing Fabergé eggs. People have been killed in their search for the eggs in the past, and to me, it's not worth a life. I'm sure it's a coincidence, the car may just be a new neighbor, but I wanted to share my father's message with you in case it could help with your research for your thesis. I'm a little spooked and hope my imagination has gotten the better of me, but if there is any truth to my father's last words, be careful with this knowledge.

May your research be fruitful,

Aleksi

"After I read that," Becca said, "I called his home but no one answered. I called the Fabergé Museum and they said Aleksi had been killed in a bicycle accident. They found his body in the street around 2:00 p.m., New York time yesterday."

Mason and RC kept quiet as they let Becca continue.

"How'd you end up at the museum?" RC asked.

"Imperial eagle's clouded case. From the poem." Becca realized RC hadn't understood the clue at all. "It refers to a Russian Imperial Presentation Gold Cigarette Case by Fabergé. The same case that's been on tour with the Fabergé exhibit that currently is displayed at the Met. I tried contacting the museum curator to see if I could get a close-up examination of the case to see if it held any clues that would be helpful for my thesis. They shut me down, and you know the rest."

Becca waited for Mason to respond, catching all the looks between him and RC. She knew they knew something, but wasn't sure what.

"Tell her," RC said to his father.

"Tell me what?" Becca looked between RC and Mason.

Mason took a deep breath and Becca could tell by the apprehensive look on Mason's face that he was about to give her some bad news.

"Ms. Lake, your contact, Aleksi, did not die in a bicycle accident.

6

"The bicycle accident was a cover-up for his murder," Mason began.

Becca's hands flew to her mouth.

"There was a puncture wound found in Aleksi's right shoulder with traces of cyanide that killed him in a matter of seconds."

"Cyanide? How do you know that?" Becca asked.

"Intelligence suggests that he was confronted not far from his home by a stranger and was bumped on his right side by the man after a brief conversation," Mason continued. "The man could've had a cyanide needle hidden in a ring. Then when Aleksi went to cross the street on his bicycle, he died in a matter of seconds before being hit by a car."

Becca put the pieces together. "If it was a cover-up, that means there had to be more than one person involved. The driver of the car had to be part of the plot to kill Aleksi in order to perfectly time it to look like an accident."

"Precisely." Mason clicked a button on his desk and the hologram in the room changed from Becca's email list to a three-dimensional satellite-projected hologram of the murder scene.

Becca gasped as she saw Aleksi's lifeless body next to his crushed bike, projected on the floor of the room as if he died right in front of her. "Who would want to kill him in such an awful way, then cover it up? From what I could tell, he was a kind man."

"The hunt for a missing Fabergé egg is not a game, Becca," RC reminded. "A single egg can be worth millions of dollars. Even Aleksi said in his email that people kill for any new piece of information."

Mason clicked another button on his desk and the projection of Aleksi's murder changed to random photos throughout the past centuries of different sketches of foxes.

"One extremist organization monitors the world for priceless artifacts. They seek and acquire precious treasures of immeasurable value like thieves in the night. They're ruthless in their methods. They're your next-door neighbors; they hide within every government and have access to your deepest, darkest secrets. Once they've acquired your scent, there's nowhere you can hide." The images morphed from the animal sketches to pencil drawings of hooded and masked men murdering villagers and stealing their valuables.

Becca didn't like looking at the creepy images. "Sounds like you're describing the boogie man."

"They're worse than him," RC added.

"Who are they?" Becca asked, "A cult?"

"A Brotherhood, in fact. Sly as a fox," Mason corrected. "Their organization has been around since the Crusades and they want what you now know."

"I'm writing a thesis, not conducting a treasure hunt," Becca exclaimed. "I have nothing of interest for this Brotherhood."

"You're wrong, very wrong. Your research has led to the death of an innocent man, and now you have the same pursuers on your tail," Mason said. "So, like it or not, Ms. Lake, your thesis has just become a valuable lead in a real treasure hunt."

"Congratulations," RC said to lighten the tension.

It didn't work. Becca felt the enormity of how much trouble she was in. She pointed to RC. "I gave him the case!"

"Which is being analyzed and decrypted by my specialists as we speak," Mason said. "The problem is that you know what's inside it and the Brotherhood of the Fox won't stop until they find you or RC to explain it to them. It doesn't matter who they get to first."

"How do I know that you're not part of this...Brotherhood of the Fox thing?"

"You'd be dead," RC said. "I thought you were smart?"

Becca grabbed a pen from Mason's desk and scribbled it from memory on a notepad.

37Prepar°er6178Ecastelet557N5gui17chet°

She ripped the page off the pad and shoved it in front of RC's face. "You tell me what this means if you're so damn smart."

RC stared at the page for a moment. "You have a photographic memory? Oh great!" He handed the page to Mason, who placed it face down on his desk. A scanner beam recorded Becca's handwriting and projected the note into the hologram in the middle of Mason's office.

RC went up to the hologram and began manipulating the cryptic message with his hands and fingers. He focused on the words first. "DIANA, highlight the most obvious words."

The hologram flickered and brought three words to everyone's attention. *Preparer, castelet, and guichet together mean prepared castle hole*, DIANA informed.

"But a hole in what castle and where?" Becca asked.

RC rearranged the words. He walked around the hologram trying to get a different perspective of the puzzle. "There are thousands of castles all over the world."

Becca thought out loud. "There's still an unused E and N. Maybe it's a different word or words that use all letters?"

"Run all known castles associated with Fabergé," Mason said.

Becca saw the hundreds of castle images flash across the room.

The program searched at a rapid pace, faster than any computer she'd seen.

RC turned toward the numbers in the hologram. "You don't think whoever left this note in the cigarette case would leave an address, do you?" RC joked.

"That's it!" Becca said with excitement. "It's a two-part message." Becca saw both RC's and Mason's blank looks. "DIANA, separate the words from the numbers, then convert the numbers to latitude and longitude."

"It's coordinates. Of course," Mason said excitedly. Both he and RC watched DIANA put the numbers in the correct order and then apply the degree symbols. It shifted the E and N from one group of numbers to the other and DIANA's search revealed one of the clue's secrets.

55.7517° N and 37.6178° E makes your destination the Kremlin in Moscow, Russia, DIANA concluded.

RC's eyes widened. "Oh...that castle."

"Well, technically, it's a palace and there are five of them," Becca corrected.

"That's great." RC's sarcasm didn't go unnoticed. "We now have a heavily guarded destination and have to find a hole in it. Plus, we don't even know what we're actually looking for."

"Yes, we do." Becca was surprised again that Mason and RC hadn't put it together yet. "Don't you see? The elephants crown the lion's gold...from Aleksi's email."

Mason sighed, obviously tired of her riddles. "Please elaborate, Ms. Lake."

"There are seven missing Fabergé eggs, but only one has both lions and an elephant on it..."

"The Royal Danish Egg," RC and Mason said at the same time.

DIANA did a quick Google search of the Royal Danish Egg and projected the images throughout the room.

Becca smiled, a bit stunned at her discovery. "The message inside the cigarette case combined with Aleksi's email tells us somewhere inside the Kremlin you'll find one of the largest handcrafted eggs by Peter Carl Fabergé." Becca felt creative satisfaction fill her body.

"DIANA, how accurate is Ms. Lake's theory here?" Mason asked.

Based on the provided evidence and mathematical numbers of probability, there's a ninety percent chance the Royal Danish Egg lies inside the Kremlin.

Becca found it a little hard to breathe. For the past year, after researching countless stories, facts, tracking hunches that led to dead ends and piecing together a crazy theory that put her on this unexpected journey, part of her had always wondered if this search was real or just a hobby. She now had her answer.

"Holy shit."

7

Winston opened the door to one of the many guest bedrooms and Becca walked inside. The word sumptuous came to mind. A blue and white comforter covered a king-sized bed. Lavender, blue, and white pillows filled one-third of the bed, and lavender and white sheets showed where the comforter had been pulled back to welcome her. Heavy drapes of the same color scheme pulled the room together, creating a cool, comfortable environment, which surprised Becca, considering the other rooms in the house were so formal.

"There are fresh clothes in the closet for you." Winston pointed with two fingers like an airline attendant doing the safety demo. "I took the liberty of preparing a warm bath. Hope you enjoy bubbles."

Becca went to the closet and looked inside. Three brand new outfits hung evenly on the rod. Each outfit had a long and a short-sleeved shirt paired with a different colored pair of jeans. Brown or black combat boots accented the outfits. "I'm not going to lie. This is a little spooky." Becca grabbed one of the shirts and looked at the size. "Looks like everything will fit perfectly. For some reason, I'm not surprised, but I do want to know how you did this."

Winston stayed by the room door and smiled. "Each room has a magic genie that lives in the closet."

Becca enjoyed Winston's sly sense of humor. "Don't you wish. Seriously though, how did you know my sizes and get clothes in my preferred style so fast? Was I scanned somewhere or something?"

"Beautiful and smart," Winston confirmed. "The moment you stepped on the front porch our security system told us everything we could possibly know. Name, age, height, weight—my wife would be very jealous, by the way—right down to your shoe size."

Becca sighed, feeling violated. "That's a massive invasion of my privacy."

"True, but it's protection for this house. When you deal in the business the Carter family does, you can never be too cautious."

"And what business is that, exactly?"

Winston smiled and conveniently didn't answer. "Should you require anything else, just press the button on the nightstand, and I or one of our staff will be with you shortly."

Becca knew there was no use in pumping Winston for information about what really went on in the house, which was more like a fortress. The amount of loyalty to the Carter family that radiated from his body was undeniable.

"There is one thing." Becca hung the outfit back up on the rod. "Do you really have a wife?"

Winston held up his left hand and showed the gold ring. "That's all I'll ever tell you about her, for her own safety." He winked and exited the room, leaving Becca to her thoughts.

She sighed when she entered the bathroom. Exhaustion washed over her as she saw the large bubble bath. It could fit at least three adults inside. She tested the water with her hand. It was the perfect temperature. Becca was impressed at the luxuriousness of the bathroom, but she was curious if the Carters appreciated it. She felt as if she was staying in a five-star hotel suite. Becca saw what appeared to be a microwave in the wall next to the tub. She studied it closer and saw the word laundry next to a light switch. She flipped the switch and a small sliding door opened, revealing a state-of-the-art laundry chute.

Place clothes inside, an automated voice said, startling Becca.

"I'm never going to get used to that," Becca said out loud. She took off her dirty, torn clothes and placed each piece in the chute. She flipped the switch and the sliding door closed. She watched her clothes get sucked upward into the wall like a vacuum cleaning a carpet.

As she stepped into the tub, Becca couldn't remember the last time she'd had a bubble bath. Her routine usually consisted of a thirty-second to a one-minute long shower. That way she could have more time to get her schoolwork done. But this...this was blissful. Becca pulled another shard of glass from her hair, then resumed relaxing in the tub. It was as if she had her own private Jacuzzi and the perfect temperature of the water enveloped her extremely sore leg muscles. The soaps were all top of the line, no real surprise there, and scents of vanilla and lavender refreshed her lungs clogged from the smell of asphalt.

Becca closed her eyes and sank down, allowing her head to be fully submerged and let her entire body relax. She felt her heartbeat slow to a more relaxed pace as she held her breath. Her mind drifted between the conscious and dream state when she heard a faint beeping noise from under the water. At first, she thought it was her head playing tricks on her but then realized it was some sort of notification alarm in the bathroom. Almost like an answering machine.

Becca reemerged from under the water and exhaled her remaining air. She wiped her hair out of her eyes and looked around for the source. To her right, she saw a flashing green light inside the rim of the tub. She tapped it and a small compartment opened as a touch screen monitor rose from inside the outer rim of the tub. The screen appeared and showed RC outside her bedroom door.

"Hello, Becca. Press and hold the light to respond," RC's voice came from the screen.

Becca pressed and held the light. "Don't come in."

RC looked up at the camera. "I can't until you unlock the door, duh. I need to talk with you. Are you dressed?"

Becca's heart sank because she didn't want to get out of the tub. "Give me a few minutes." She tapped the light and the screen descended back inside the rim of the tub. She got out of the bath and grabbed the nearest towel from the warming rack. Becca took a quick moment allowing the towel to warm her like a comfortable blanket before wiping off the excess bubbles. She grabbed the bathrobe hanging on the back of the bathroom door, quickly put it on, and went to the bedroom door to see what the hell RC wanted.

RC didn't wait to be let in. He just waltzed right into her room like he owned the place when she opened the door. She saw him casting a few glances at her in the bathrobe.

"What do you want?"

"New phone, tablet, and laptop, as promised." He placed each item on her bed. "They've been encrypted so the Brotherhood won't be able to access anything you do on any device without having the proper passcodes that are connected to our servers. All your contacts, emails, videos, and pics have also been restored."

"Thanks, but I just needed the new phone since you ditched my last one," Becca replied.

"You're going to need more than your phone in Russia."

"I'm going to Russia? I thought you were."

"Not by myself. My father has demanded you come with me. I think it's stupid, but he's the boss."

Becca had always wanted to go to Russia although she'd imagined it would be under completely different circumstances. Plus, there was another issue preventing her from going. "I don't have a passport."

"You do now." RC handed her one in a leather case.

She opened it and saw a professionally taken photo of her face.

All her vital information was correctly included and from the way it felt, the passport was completely legitimate. "I didn't take this. How did you get it?"

RC just looked at her and she knew that somehow, they had their way of doing things.

"This is too weird," Becca exclaimed.

"That's not weird. The fact that I have to watch over a baby is weird," RC said.

She couldn't believe it. The insults just kept coming from this jerk.

"Look," Becca began with her blood boiling again, "I'm not going to apologize for getting involved in something I wasn't even aware was happening. So, I'd appreciate it if you could refrain from your constant insults for two seconds and allow me to process what's going on."

RC put his hands up, confused. "What are you so offended about?"

"Don't call me a baby," she protested.

"Oh, for God's sake. It's code," RC explained. "Baby is the term we use to identify an innocent bystander in my line of work. So, chill."

Becca wasn't expecting that and felt a little embarrassed. "So back at the hotel room when you said you had a baby that needs a nest, you meant a safe house."

"Now you're getting it. Good for you." His annoyance with her didn't go unnoticed. "Since you're a baby going into the field, there are a few rules to follow. If you deviate from these said rules, chances are you will not be returning. Comprendé?"

Becca wondered how much longer she could tolerate his superior attitude. In this matter, he was superior to her, but she was developing a serious problem with his authority. "Okay, your Majesty."

RC glared at her impertinence. "One. No questioning of me when things get heated and believe me, they will."

Becca attempted to speak but his voice grew louder to overpower hers. "Two. If I say run, you run and don't look back." His eyes were so intense she felt as if she was going off to war. "Three." He grabbed her phone and held it up. "Your phone has an emergency extraction button on the right side. You only use this button if it is life or death. When you press it, follow the instructions to the letter. If the enemy takes one of us, you use it to get out. Response time is five minutes." He handed the phone back to her. "And last but not least, we'll be working closely together, so bring the bathrobe." His blunt delivery startled her.

"Is that it?" She ignored his last comment.

"Are you a black belt by any chance? Martial arts experience? Anything that could be useful in the field if things go wrong?"

"I helped my best friend at a bake sale once." She enjoyed the deflation on RC's face.

"I can't believe this." He headed for the door. "Get dressed," RC said. "We leave in an hour."

Becca could tell he was not happy.

"Welcome to the world of treasure hunting." RC left and slammed the door behind him.

"Thanks for the pep talk," Becca said.

8

Becca would have preferred to fly through the stars under different circumstances. She'd never flown in a private jet before, and this brand-new Gulfstream G700 was incredible. The jet flew at fifty-thousand feet, had four large cabins with room for a crew compartment, up to nineteen seated passengers and could sleep up to ten passengers. The front was the large galley and a lavatory. The next cabin, where she sat, had seats positioned two-by-two that were separated by the center aisle. Two settees were down the right and left sides of the plane behind the rows of seats. A separate cabin was a conference room and the rear cabin was actually a master bedroom with a shower.

A flight attendant catered to her every need but Becca declined the offer of alcohol and stayed with an assortment of gourmet cheeses, crackers, sparkling water, and coffee. Somehow, the Carters even had her favorite brand, Starbucks Verona, on board. If it'd been daylight, the large panoramic windows would have shown a spectacular view but Becca knew she couldn't enjoy it due to her current situation. She felt the crosshairs on her back now. Being hunted by an ancient organization was not something she ever thought she'd experience and she wondered if the fear would ever go away.

Becca sipped the brew as she sat in her seat and searched the Internet on the tray table's built-in computer, looking for any mention of the Brotherhood of the Fox. She glanced behind her and saw RC in the conference room, not sure what he was working on.

"Well, you seem to be doing all right." Barry's sarcasm wasn't difficult to miss, even through the Skype session on Becca's monitor.

She returned her attention to her screen. Seeing Barry's apartment full of computers made her wish she was there with him and surrounded by something familiar.

"I'm better now that I know you're okay," she said.

"Who said I was?" Barry replied quickly. "I've never been shot at, chased, or almost run over before. Even the police couldn't do much because I couldn't identify the men in suits or their identical black cars."

"Things are a little crazy right now, Barry," Becca agreed.

"I wonder if the government found out about my hack of NASA two years ago?" Barry asked. Becca saw he was still shaken because he couldn't sit still. "Coming after me like that is a bit extreme, don't you think?"

Becca didn't respond. She wanted to tell Barry about the Brotherhood, but couldn't bring herself to tell him, as she didn't believe it herself. His fingers constantly tapped his desk and the repeated clicking distracted her. Becca heard a computer beep from Barry's end. His computer finished a cross-reference search.

"No match. My command center needs more info if you want a better chance at pinpointing the location of where the egg could be."

"This is hopeless." Becca placed her face in her hands. "I've gone through every scrap of information I pulled together over the past year in my head. There's no mention anywhere of the egg appearing or being near the Kremlin." She focused on the open, scanned documents on her monitor. She had pulled up three pages of very old articles from the Russian Revolution in 1918. Each had the word "yaytso" which translated to "egg" in English. It wasn't much to go on but she was hoping that with the information discovered from Aleksi, these articles were referring to the Royal Danish Egg, however unlikely.

"Don't say another word, Becca," RC interrupted. He leaned over her and clicked a button on the keyboard, which cut off the Skype session with Barry.

"What the hell did you do that for?" Becca exclaimed. "That was incredibly rude! He's my best friend and helping us."

"And we're helping him by having him not know exactly what we plan to do. He's a baby. The less he knows the safer he is."

Again, he was right. Becca had fallen into her habit of contacting Barry when she needed help. He knew lots of fancy tricks to do with computers. She didn't.

"You can't involve innocent people in your search when it comes to the Brotherhood," RC explained. "If they can't get to you right away, they will get to your friends and family first, then you. It's basic safety. Stop being so careless."

Becca didn't mean to be careless. She was focused on discovering more about the mysterious organization that had almost killed her and Barry. "I was only trying to get ahead of the game."

"That's not how you do it," he said. Becca knew it was RC's way of making sure she understood to never do that again. "You need to start getting used to keeping secrets, even from your boyfriend."

"He's not my—"

"Where did you get that?" RC interrupted, staring at her screen, seeing one of her research papers. His surprised tone caught her attention.

"When I was researching my thesis months ago. What's the problem?"

RC pointed to a smudge on the top left corner of the document. "Zoom in on that."

Becca did and the smudge had a few scratch-looking marks that created the outline of a weird animal face. "What's that?"

"That's an old symbol used by the Brotherhood of the Fox," RC confirmed.

A sudden burst of energy surged through Becca's body. "You're kidding." Becca peered closer to her screen. "That tiny thing?"

"DIANA, add up how many documents from Becca's research have that emblem," RC said.

Becca watched over three hundred documents get scanned on her screen right before her eyes. She was startled at first, then not surprised that the fancy DIANA computer system was on the Carter family plane.

She realized her right leg was bouncing rapidly. The scent of RC's cologne reached her nose. It had a hint of musk, which she found incredibly sexy until she remembered who the wearer was.

"Could you take a step back, please? You're crowding me and I'm trying to focus."

"I'm glad you like my cologne," RC said confidently.

She hated he could see through her deceptions.

Eighty-five research papers have the emblem, DIANA said, helping Becca refocus on the task at hand.

"Now have the computer extract all names from the documents," Becca said as DIANA inputted the information.

"What exactly are you trying to do?" RC asked.

"If there are any names on the pages with the emblem, it's easy to assume that those people were somehow involved with the Brotherhood."

"I'm not following. You think finding people's names will help you locate the egg?" RC asked.

"Someone put the egg in the Kremlin. It didn't just magically appear there. It has to be someone who worked in the Kremlin or someone who had access inside."

RC caught on. "Someone the Brotherhood might've been hunting."

Seven names, DIANA informed.

"Check if any of those people ever worked at the Kremlin."

Three people, DIANA said. *Viktor Sokolov, Dmitry Petrov, and Oleg Bogatir.*

"Oh my God. That's it," Becca gasped.

"Could Oleg Bogatir be related to your contact?" RC asked.

"It must be his grandfather. How else would Aleksi learn about the egg?"

RC was already ahead of her thinking. "DIANA, do a background check for a Kremlin employee from 1930 through 1945 named Oleg Bogatir."

The familiar automated voice replied throughout the cabin. *Searching.* Becca waited a few moments, trying to focus and not think about RC's cologne.

Oleg Bogatir was a construction worker for the Grand Kremlin Palace. He was commissioned to repair old buildings and part of the wall along the Kremlin embankment. He was survived by his son, Ivan Bogatir, and his grandson, Aleksi Bogatir, DIANA replied.

Becca sat back in her seat and exhaled a sigh of relief. She looked at RC. "We just narrowed down our search."

"There's still a problem," RC said, "Where, and in what wall of the Kremlin? Good job on narrowing down the person involved with the egg, but we're still talking about infiltrating the Kremlin. I'm not wasting money on this op without hard facts. I need more information. I can get us inside, but I will only do so when I know I can get us out safely."

RC was right. With what they knew, they were still on a wild goose chase.

"Exactly how do you propose to even get inside the Kremlin?" Becca asked.

"You focus on what you do, I'll focus on what I do," RC said.

Becca's phone buzzed with a text. It was from Barry and read, "Are you sure you can trust this trust fund baby?" Barry's jealous tone was clear even through text messaging.

"As soon as we're done here, he can gladly have you back," RC said, having read Barry's text.

"You didn't have to cut him off so abruptly. No wonder nobody likes you."

"That's not true." RC smiled, sure of himself. "People love me."

Becca wanted to smack the cockiness right out of him.

RC turned to go to the conference room and said, "Trust me, your boyfriend is safer not knowing what we're up to."

"For the last time," Becca said following RC, "He's not my boyfriend."

"He wants to be." RC's attention didn't leave the laptop he worked on as he walked back to the conference table.

"No, he doesn't. I've known him most of my life."

RC looked directly at her. "No straight man puts his life on hold or is willing to break the law by hacking into databases to help his," he held up his fingers like the quotation sign, "friend" break into the Kremlin."

Becca had never thought about Barry that way. He was always there for her, but like the brother she'd never had. Plus, he'd never given any sign of romantic interest, or she'd never noticed.

"I really don't think he's your type anyway," RC stated factually as he returned his attention to the computer.

Becca sighed, annoyed, and wanted to change the subject.

It dawned on her. "Aleksi's dad! That's where we start." She looked at RC. "Aleksi's dad told him the poem on his deathbed. There's a good chance that he had more information."

The P.A. came on, "We're now making our descent into Sheremetyevo Airport, Mr. Carter."

9

After nine hours, Becca stepped off the Gulfstream into a chilly morning temperature of fifty-two degrees and light rain. The gray gloom added to the mystique of the Russian capital of Moscow. After clearing Customs, a private car drove them to Aleksi's father's apartment.

They parked around the corner to avoid suspicion by local residents. It had been less than a week since Aleksi and his father passed away. Becca recognized the street corner where she had seen the image of Aleksi's lifeless body projected in Mason's office. It wigged her out that she was walking down the same street.

They arrived at Aleksi's father's apartment building. RC tested the door handle. Locked. He looked back at Becca.

"You'd be surprised how many people leave their doors unlocked." RC pulled out his picks. "Act like you're looking for the keys."

Becca did as requested and fished through her coat pockets. People walked down the sidewalk, not paying them any attention. Click. RC opened the door and both he and Becca entered the building.

"The second floor," RC said quietly.

She followed his lead. If she had learned anything in the past thirty-six hours, it was to let RC do what he did best. She was a novice when it came to an actual treasure hunt.

"This one," RC said as they arrived at the door. Becca was fascinated at how skilled RC was at picking locks.

A neighbor's front door opened and, in a flash, RC grabbed Becca, quickly pushed her back up against the door, and placed his head close to her neck.

"Rub your hands through my hair, quickly," he whispered in her ear.

Frightened, startled, and confused, Becca gently placed her hands on the back of RC's head. She saw the neighbor exit the apartment and stare at them. It all made sense to her. The neighbor thought RC and Becca were getting it on. If he only knew what Becca was feeling behind her. Wrapped around Becca's waist, RC's hands were slowly continuing to pick the lock of Aleksi's father's front door, completely out of sight from the neighbor.

Becca watched the neighbor uncomfortably walk by them and give them privacy. The neighbor quickly descended the staircase.

"Becca," RC said quietly.

"Yeah?" Her eyes were still looking at the staircase making sure the neighbor didn't return.

"Becca," RC said with more of a stern tone.

"What?" she said quietly.

"The door is unlocked."

Becca immediately let go of his head, embarrassed, realizing she had been lingering. He was still face-to-face with her and she saw his captivating blue eyes beautifully staring back at her.

"Your pupils are dilated," he said.

"What?" She tried to come up with an excuse. "Must be all the coffee I had on the plane."

"May I?" he asked, motioning for her to move.

"Yes, sorry." She slid to the side, completely embarrassed, and felt her heart beating fast in her chest.

RC opened the door. Becca pulled herself together and followed him inside.

The apartment was ransacked, chairs were toppled over or broken, the couch cushions were shredded, bookshelves had fallen on the floor with books and knickknacks scattered all over the room.

"Clearly, we're in the right place," RC said.

"This is weird." Becca looked around the room, "It's almost as if this mess is designed to look like a struggle happened. It's staged."

"Not bad. The Brotherhood is very thorough when orchestrating cover-ups," RC confirmed.

Images flashed in Becca's mind, forming and reforming to deduce how the condo destruction happened based on the layout of the mess.

"It was one person." She walked up to the fallen bookshelf and found a faint footprint in the dust. "Male, from the looks of the tread in the thick dust."

"Two men," RC corrected, "There's another footprint on the other side."

Becca looked at the other footprint, which was more visible than the first. It was the exact same size. Becca shook her head. "One male, not two," she corrected with absolute certainty. "That's the same footprint conveniently placed to appear as if there were two intruders."

"Very good." RC smiled. Becca knew by his change in body language she had been right and he'd been testing her. "This would be a lot easier if we knew exactly what we were looking for." RC's impatient tone didn't go unnoticed. "Based on this mess, I bet he got what he wanted."

Becca moved to the bedroom and saw the bed ripped to shreds, lamps shattered on the floor, dresser drawers pulled out and emptied.

"I disagree. Based on the violent destruction of the bedroom compared to the living room, I don't think they found it. This mess is born from anger, which says to me the intruder was getting frustrated, and the only reason he'd be frustrated was because he didn't find what he was looking for. But there's only a forty percent chance I'm right."

"You got to that conclusion by looking at a bedroom?" RC asked slightly impressed.

"Yeah. I think in terms of probabilities and draw conclusions." Becca saw a broken white ceramic statue of Pegasus on the bedroom floor. Normally she wouldn't have paid much attention to it but there was an inconsistency in the design of the left-wing. "RC," Becca called, "What do you make of this?"

RC saw the broken statue on the ground. "I'd say you've found a broken statute."

"No," Becca sighed, pointing to the wing on the ground. "Look closely at the pattern of the feathers. What do you see?"

RC moved closer to the wing. "Four of the feathers' design details are opposite from the rest of the wing."

"Why is that?" Becca pointed.

RC quickly picked up the broken wing and pulled off the four feathers that had been stuck to the statue with some kind of glue. "That's because these feathers belong in a different place." RC immediately searched the bedroom.

"What's going on? How do you know it belongs somewhere else?" Becca asked confused.

"Someone in Aleksi's family worked for the same organization I do." He held up the ceramic feathers. "This is a key. Our protocol mandates that members must store their secret identities or valuables in a hidden compartment in one of three places. Look for an indentation that matches the key on the mantle in the living room or the side of the tub in the bathroom, and I'll check the bedroom walls."

"If someone in Aleksi's family was a member of your organization, that explains how he knew the cryptic poem. So, does that mean Aleksi was also part of your group?"

"Not necessarily," RC responded from the bedroom. "Sometimes one person in a family is a member and the others have no idea. Secrecy is always key, even among family members. But my guess is Oleg, the grandfather, was the member."

Becca headed for the bathroom. "So, are you going to tell me what organization you work for, or are you going to make me guess?"

"You know I'm not supposed to say anything, Becca," RC said from the bedroom. "The less you know the better, but I'm surprised you haven't figured it out already with how observant you are."

The modern bathroom wasn't as trashed as the rest of the condo, mainly because there wasn't much to trash in the first place. A few medicine bottles were scattered on the counter, sink, and floor. Becca traced her fingers along the bathroom tub, searching for the indentation.

"Okay then…your technology access is beyond military-grade, which means you and the organization you work for have deeper connections than the standard government level. That explains how you were released from being arrested after stealing the cigarette case back at the museum." She finished searching the tub and found nothing.

"Actually, I didn't steal it, remember?" he corrected.

Becca moved to the mantle in the living room and continued her deductions while searching for the indentation. "I noticed the tiny brand of a claw on the inside of your right wrist when we first met. I didn't think anything of it until I was in your father's office and noticed his ring bore the symbol of a griffin. Nowadays, men wear class rings from college as reminders and achievements; his ring was ceremonial looking or established some sort of rank. Given his authoritative presence and mall of a house, he is the head of your organization and since I am still alive it's clear your organization isn't into thieving and murder like the other one.

"You, against your will, have been ordered to keep me safe," she continued. "That means you are a protector and the griffin is a symbol of protection. Since you work in the business of recovering lost treasures, I'd say you are the Anti-Brotherhood of treasure hunters. I just don't know what to call your organization. The Brotherhood of Griffins?" She felt four grooves on the right side of the mantle. "I found it," she hollered to RC, who rushed into the living room with the key.

"We prefer the term League," RC said as he placed the ceramic feather key against the indentation in the side of the mantle and pushed the key like a button. *Click.* "The League of Griffins." A hidden drawer popped open in the front of the mantle. Both Becca and RC moved to the drawer to see what was inside.

"The League of Griffins?" Becca clarified. "Sounds like a comic book."

"I wasn't born during the Crusades when the organization was formed. So, I didn't name us." RC pulled the drawer fully out of the mantle and carried it to the overturned kitchen table.

Becca stood the table upright for RC to place the drawer on top. Inside the drawer was a dirty, large, manila envelope that hadn't been opened in what appeared to be decades. RC opened the clasp and pulled out a folded sheet depicting faded architectural designs of a Russian tower.

"It's too faded to read." Becca gazed at the drawings. "It doesn't say what tower it is."

"I think I have an app for that." RC pulled out his phone, pressed an app, and began scanning the document. "The scan goes back to headquarters and can easily be recreated digitally on our servers. Should take about thirty seconds for Dad to receive it and a few more seconds for DIANA to process it."

Becca continued to pore over the blueprints to get as much information as she could. "Look at this." She pointed to a section of the tower. "These are construction plans for filling some sort of wall with concrete. Aleksi's father made a special design on this side of the wall. It looks like a small gap or opening."

Both Becca and RC gazed at the small gap design.

"That's got to be our hole in the wall," RC said.

"We still don't know what tower this is in the Kremlin. It'd be a cinch if the words hadn't faded."

"Not to worry, by the time we arrive at the rendezvous point HQ should have narrowed down which tower it is. Let's go."

Becca put the blueprints back in the old envelope as RC returned the drawer to the mantle.

RC checked his phone. "The driver is bringing the car around now."

Becca headed to the front door. "Where are we going?" she asked RC as she opened it.

She gasped.

Staring back at her was a man dressed in all black, from combat boots to his hood, wearing a terrifying gray and white mask shaped like a fox head.

10

"Becca, MOVE!" RC shoved Becca out of the way to dodge the masked man's knife thrust. She lost her footing and fell to the wood floor, dropping the manila envelope. Thuds, grunts, and violent whooshes filled the apartment. Becca pushed up from the floor and looked back to process what the hell just happened.

She watched RC viciously defend himself against the masked man, dodging his knife attacks. RC kicked his opponent back and the two had a quick moment to analyze each other before resuming their brawl. The masked man was incredibly skilled and appeared better trained in the art of close-quarters combat than RC. The assassin sliced at RC with astonishing accuracy, barely missing his target. RC blocked a strike, trapped his opponent's hands with his own, and twisted, forcing the assassin to drop the knife. RC kicked the knife out of reach and was shoved down next to the fireplace by his attacker. The masked man pulled a smaller knife out from behind his back and threw it at RC.

Becca gasped as she watched RC roll out of the way, barely clearing the knife's path as it stuck in the wood floor and vibrated from the force of the throw. The assassin advanced on RC, who quickly grabbed the fireplace poker and jumped to his feet. RC swung the poker like he was wielding a sword with exquisite precision. The assassin defended himself against RC's attacks. RC forced the assassin to move back into the bedroom hallway. Becca cautiously followed them, desperately looking for a way to help. She saw the knife and snatched it up. She was making up the plan on the spot and knew she had to come up with something fast.

RC swung the poker at the assassin over and over again but his opponent wasn't an easy target to hit. RC went for a side slice but the poker got caught under one of the shelves and the assassin took advantage of the situation.

Becca watched the masked man grab RC, ram him into the hallway wall, and knee him multiple times in the stomach. Grunting, RC used his body weight and tackled the assassin into the opposite wall, elbowing him in the mask. The assailant threw RC into the bedroom, breaking down the door.

Becca saw an opportunity and threw the knife at the assassin's back. She knew the probability of hitting her opponent was above seventy percent because the hallway was narrow and her target was a big man. What she didn't know was if the knife would hit properly.

In a swift move, the masked assassin turned around and caught the knife by the handle.

"Don't help!" RC yelled from the bedroom as he got up to his feet.

The assassin faced RC and charged. RC grabbed the nearest lamp on the nightstand and used it as a weapon to defend against the continuous knife thrusts. He found an opening and clocked the assassin in the head with the lamp, breaking its base and the bulb. The assassin took a couple of steps back, stunned, and attempted to shake it off, but RC wasn't letting up. Becca desperately wanted to help RC but knew she was no match for the situation.

RC smashed the assassin's head into the wall mirror, shattering glass everywhere. The man fell to the ground, RC grabbed one of the assassin's knives from his belt and held it to the man's neck.

Becca covered her mouth in fear as she watched the two men struggle on the floor to gain control of the knife.

The assassin resisted with all his strength, pushing against RC, but RC had gravity and leverage. RC used his body weight to drive the knife into the assassin's neck, instantly killing him. The moment RC's opponent stopped moving he scrambled off the body.

Becca hurried over to a heavily breathing RC and noticed his left forearm had a long gash. "You're bleeding." She grabbed a pillow, removed the covering, and wrapped it around his gash to stop the bleeding.

"I'm okay," he reassured her. He got to his feet, walked over to the assassin's body, and removed the fox mask revealing the attacker's true face.

"That's the neighbor from down the hall!" Becca gasped.

"The Brotherhood is everywhere, remember?" RC replied. "I think we've overstayed our welcome." He pulled out his phone and made a call. "I need a bath A.S.A.P. Confirm five minutes." He hung up. "Becca, we've gotta go."

Becca stared at the assassin's face and the fox mask next to it. The man had to be in his late thirties and had a kind face, which terrified her as it really sank in that the kindest people around could be killers.

"Becca, come on!" RC prodded. He grabbed her arm and escorted her out of the apartment, stopping to pick up the blueprints she had dropped at the front door.

11

Becca and RC walked down the sidewalk as casually as possible, which wasn't very casual at all. They came to their car and found the driver with his head on the steering wheel, asleep.

Becca went toward the car but RC hooked his arm through hers and continued walking down the sidewalk away from the car. "That's our car back there," she said.

"That was our car." RC kept calm as they continued walking away. "We're compromised."

"But the driver's in there," Becca exclaimed.

"He's not sleeping, Becca. He's dead," RC said bluntly.

Becca gasped.

"The assassin went to the car first before returning to deal with us."

"What if it was someone else?" Becca asked, concerned.

"I'd rather not stick around to find out," he said as they turned the corner.

They searched for a public place to hide in plain sight where another fox assassin would be less likely to attack. Twenty-five minutes later Becca and RC sat outside at a random street café they'd found. Tons of people went about their day and cars crowded the street. The smell of sweet pastries was a comforting distraction after the horrific event back at the apartment. Becca sat at the table quietly with her arms folded in front of her. Her hair blew in the slight wind and she shivered from the adrenaline running throughout her body.

RC had ordered tea for both of them to shake the nerves, but Becca's tea remained untouched in front of her. The sweet vanilla honey smell was inviting, but she wasn't ready to take a sip yet. RC had already finished his tea. He checked his phone again.

"Is this the first time you've ever killed someone?" Becca quietly asked, not sure how she would react to the coming answer.

"Does it matter?" RC responded without looking away from his phone. She envied his calm demeanor and didn't understand how he could be so casual after such a traumatic experience.

"I don't know," Becca replied honestly, "Never thought I'd witness, let alone be part of, a murder. Is it murder if it's self-defense?"

"Self-defense is self-defense," he said, still not looking away from his phone. "Drink your tea."

Becca picked up the cup and took a very small sip. Her eyes saw a security camera pointed right at them. "Shouldn't we still be moving? I don't think this is the best spot to be."

"Don't worry about the cameras." He held up his phone, "I'm jamming them right now. We have ten minutes of safety."

"How do you figure that?"

"Basic training. When being pursued, don't run...walk, blend with the crowd, and don't stay in any one place longer than ten minutes."

Becca took another sip of her tea and returned the cup to its saucer. She hesitated before asking, "Can you teach me?"

RC put his phone on the table and looked her right in the eyes for the first time since they sat in the café. "If we get out of Russia alive."

"Can you make sure that happens?" She knew she was asking an impossible request, but needed some sort of reassurance.

"It's my job."

The confidence in RC's voice was comforting. After what she had witnessed back in the apartment with the assassin and how skilled RC was, she felt a tiny glimmer of hope that they'd make it back to the States.

RC's phone vibrated on the table. He looked at it and then looked at a taxi pulling up to the curb. "That's our ride." He left some rubles on the table and they both walked to the cab. RC opened the door for Becca, allowing her to get in first.

The overcast skies of Moscow only added to Becca's melancholy. She gazed out the window not looking at the sights, but at the people. Men, women, and children of all ages, sizes, nationalities, and professions, all perfectly ordinary, and all possible assassins for the Brotherhood of the Fox. She saw a bicyclist with a backpack and wondered if it contained one of those terrifying fox masks.

She knew she'd never be able to look at people the same way again. She feared she wouldn't be able to see a person's genuine kindness without seeing their potential threat. No one was an innocent bystander anymore.

The cab came to a stop. RC exited and paid the driver through the driver's side window. Becca exited and saw where they were.

"The Russian State Library?" she asked as she gazed at the massive pillars that lined the building.

RC walked past her. "We're not here to check out a book," he said and headed up the concrete stairs.

Becca had never seen such an enormous library in person. Beautiful multicolored marble pillars decorated the Russian State Library. Bronze busts, elegant ornate lighting fixtures, and the scent of dusty books gave the library a slightly operatic feel without being overly dramatic.

"Keep up, Becca," RC said from almost twenty feet away.

Becca double-timed her steps to catch up to RC, who clearly

didn't care about the library's architecture. They entered a card catalog room.

"Stop," a woman's voice said in English with a Russian accent.

Becca and RC turned around to see a gorgeous blonde woman, slender, early thirties, walk up to them. "May I help you find something?" she asked her attention only on RC.

"Only if you have the wings needed to assist."

Becca saw the flirtatious look in the librarian's eyes. At first, it seemed like the strangest response to the worst pick-up line she'd ever heard, until the librarian reached out her right hand and revealed a small brand of a wing on the inside of her wrist.

"And whom do I have the pleasure of escorting?" the librarian asked.

RC rolled up his right sleeve, revealing the branded claw on his wrist.

"Satisfied?" RC asked.

"Right this way, Mr. Carter." The librarian smiled.

Becca was surprised by the feeling of annoyance that flashed through her from the librarian's flirtatious attitude toward RC. What bothered her the most was RC's acceptance of it. That, mixed with the confusion of why the hell they were there, didn't do anything for her nerves.

"Do you want to ask for her number, or should I just hand her your room key?" Becca asked.

"We have a job to do, Becca, focus please."

"And where does undressing her with your eyes come in to the job?"

"If you got it, flaunt it," RC smirked. "No shame in that."

Becca gritted her teeth, not having a witty comeback. They followed the librarian to the reading room, where they met three large men in trench coats. They each showed their brand, a talon, on their right wrists, then bowed their heads to RC.

"Wait here until we're done," RC said to Becca.

"Done with what? I'm not exactly sure what's going on," Becca replied.

RC faced the librarian. "Please see to all my friend's needs while I'm away."

The librarian nodded with the most flirtatious smile that made Becca want to gag. The woman didn't even try to hide her interest in RC.

"You can't leave me alone with her. I thought we were sticking together in this." Becca didn't like having a babysitter.

RC immediately grabbed both her arms and shook her lightly. Then he looked directly into her eyes and said, "You're safe here. We own the place."

The librarian pressed a hidden button on the closest wall and it quietly opened to show an entrance to a private conference room.

Becca saw the button had the same winged griffin design as the button on the mantle back in the apartment. She looked at RC, finally understanding what was going on. They were in a safe house, or safe library.

"Oh. Why didn't you say that in the first place?"

"That kind of defeats the purpose of a secret organization," RC replied and walked inside the conference room with the three other men.

The librarian closed the door behind them and faced her. "How long have you been with Mr. Carter?"

The librarian's fishing was obvious. "I met him yesterday."

"You're a very lucky girl. Their meeting may take a few hours. I'm supposed to keep you in this room not far from Mr. Carter. May I get you anything to pass the time?"

"Can you get me any books that have layouts of the Kremlin from the 1930s up to today?"

The librarian nodded, took out her cell phone, and texted the request. "They will be brought to you shortly. Please have a seat."

Becca sat down at one of the many reading tables in the room. She pored through book after book, not leaving much space on the table, devouring as much information as she could. She looked up and saw the librarian sitting at the table across from her texting on the phone.

After about an hour of looking through the books, Becca narrowed down the ones that had different blueprints and layouts of the Kremlin. There were at least ten she believed might help her piece together the faded letters on the map left behind by Aleksi's father. RC had taken the actual map into his meeting, but that wasn't enough to stop Becca.

"Is there a piece of paper and pencil around here?" Becca asked, clearly interrupting the librarian from her texting.

The librarian left, then returned with a pad of paper and a pen for Becca. The shade the librarian threw in her direction didn't go unnoticed. Becca assumed the negative attitude had to do with some misplaced sense of jealousy from the woman, probably because Becca was hanging around RC and being protected by him. If only the librarian truly knew what Becca thought of him. Although, part of her enjoyed having a gorgeous woman be jealous of her.

Becca quickly drew a bird's eye view of Aleksi's father's map from memory. Once completed, she searched through each Kremlin layout, mixing, and matching certain towers to her drawing, looking for similarities to fill in the faded words on the map. It was like putting a puzzle together. The starting point always takes the longest, but if you begin at the edges, the center usually falls into place. This was the same principle. Only the edges were the Kremlin towers. Match the layout; find the name of the tower. Just twenty towers in the Kremlin to mix and match with over seventy-six years' worth of modifications. No problem.

Any concept of time quickly disappeared as Becca dug deeper and deeper into her scavenger hunt for the correct tower. Passageways would match one side of the map but not the other. Becca looked through book after book, getting through about half of them before she found a match, or at least seventy-five percent of a match. Modifications had been made in the book that didn't necessarily match the map, but the number of similarities couldn't be ignored. Becca even turned the book and the map drawing upside down and moved them in different directions to prove her theory to herself. She felt excitement feed her adrenaline and her focus as she did her best to contain herself before jumping to the wrong conclusion.

Becca wrote down the names of certain passageways on the map, based on the book layout, leaving others unmarked. Once all the passageway names from the book were on the map, she repeated the process, mixing and matching with other books from different time periods.

She was on a roll. Before she knew it, she had filled in all the names of all the passageways that led to the Tainitskaya Tower, also more commonly known as the Secret Tower. Typical.

Becca sat back in her chair and looked at her fully labeled, hand-drawn map of the Secret Tower and now understood what it meant. She could easily see where a gap in a well at the bottom of the tower had been filled with concrete and now knew the route to get there.

"A hole in a castle wall…or in this case, the Secret Tower in the Kremlin," she muttered quietly, proud of herself for solving the riddle.

The bigger problem was figuring out how to get inside the Kremlin. Her phone vibrated.

It was a Facetime call from her mother. Becca folded up her map, plugged in her headphones, and walked over to the corner to answer the call. The librarian followed Becca, which didn't surprise her in the least. She answered the call and saw her mom appear on her iPhone screen with a black eye and a fat, cut lip. Becca's heart sank, disgusted with how her mother looked.

"I see Dad came back."

12

"It's honestly not as bad as it looks, sweetheart," her mom said as she placed a bag of ice on her fat lip.

"I'm calling the police." Becca had had it with seeing her mother post-beatings.

"Don't do that, Becca."

"Mom, your face is swollen! He deserves to be in jail. Why do you let him keep doing this to you?"

"One day you'll understand."

"There's nothing to understand!" Becca struggled to keep her voice down, remembering she was in a library. "You should never let that creep in the house!"

"He's my husband and he pays for this house."

"Why do you always defend him? After years of this, it doesn't make any sense. All you have to do is press charges and he goes away for good. He won't be able to hurt you anymore. It's so simple!"

"That's not me."

Becca wished she could strangle some sense into her mother. Why this sweet woman put up with such an abusive husband was something she knew she'd never understand.

"Mom, you have to stand up for yourself at this point. You can't keep letting him do this to you. He'll kill you one day."

It was as if her logical reasoning was deflected by some imaginary shield that surrounded her mother from common sense.

"He loves me," her mother said softly, "in his own way."

"It's a good thing I wasn't there when he returned. I would've broken his legs."

"If you were here, he would've harmed you worse than me. The only way to get him to leave is to let him do what he wants."

She couldn't believe what her mother was saying. "How many more beatings are you willing to take? I can't stand to see you this way, Mom. Tell me, why do you allow this?"

"You and Barry having a good time?" her mom asked.

It was classic deflection. Becca's mom always changed the subject when she wouldn't answer a tough question.

"Things are great. Nothing too exciting," she lied.

"That's good, and how's the research for the thesis coming?"

Becca had no idea how she would explain to her mother that she was currently in Russia and people had already tried to kill her. "I think I've bitten off more than I can chew, to be honest."

"You'll figure it out, I'm sure. You always do," her mother said. "I just wanted to see you, tell you I love you, honey, and wanted to let you know that I'm okay."

"I love you too, but you're not okay. Go to the hospital."

"Good luck with your research, I'm proud of you." Her mom ended the Facetime session.

"Mom...Mom!" Becca hated not being able to get through to her mother. Hated it.

"Damn it, Mom. You're better than this," she mumbled to herself. She exhaled her frustration and felt tears forming in her eyes. She desperately wanted to help her mother get away from her abusive father but didn't see how she could with her mother's denials about the situation. She could only open the door so far; her mother had to cross the threshold.

The secret doorway to the conference room opened and out walked RC and the three other men.

"It's in the—" RC started.

"Secret Tower," Becca finished.

The look of surprise on RC's face was refreshing to Becca.

"How did you...?"

Becca handed RC her map with the completed names of the towers along the Kremlin wall. "I had some time to kill while you chatted. With the help of a few books, I put the puzzle together to complete the map we'd found." She caught how impressed RC was even though he tried to hide it.

"Photographic memory, remember?" She pointed to the map. "I found there's a a hidden passageway at the bottom of the Secret Tower with a well in it. Hence the name of the tower," she said wryly. "There's an exit from the passageway that was blocked and the well was filled in sometime in the 1930s. That would be a good time for Aleksi's grandfather to have hidden a priceless artifact, don't you think?"

"Not a bad thought," RC handed the map back to Becca. "You all right?" he asked looking closely at her.

Becca hesitated. She hadn't fully shaken the emotions of the Facetime chat with her mother and she sure as hell wasn't going to tell RC about it. "Just getting hungry."

"We're done here." He turned to the three guys. "Bring the car around." The three men nodded their heads and walked away. The librarian walked up to RC and handed him a small piece of paper. He opened it.

Becca rolled her eyes when she saw it was the librarian's phone number. "I'm starving," she exclaimed just to snap RC out of the moment.

RC smiled at the librarian.

Becca gave the woman the cheesiest smile. "It was nice meeting you," she said as she wrapped her arm through RC's. "Thanks for the notepad and pen." She left the room with him.

"Jealous?" RC asked.

"Not in the least. I just don't like her."

As soon as they were out of the librarian's sight, Becca let go of RC and kept an arm's length distance from him. No doubt he was confused.

"I don't get you girls."

"You never will," she confirmed.

Becca and RC exited the library to a beautiful setting sun in the distance. The gray sky had cleared to a bright blue while they'd been inside. The temperature had dropped a bit and Becca shivered. They walked to the parked passenger van waiting for them. One of the three men from RC's meeting opened the rear door for Becca and RC to enter. It wasn't lost on Becca how annoyed she was with the adoration RC continued to receive. She had always wanted a personal chauffeur and a strapping bodyguard to accompany her, but not under life-and-death circumstances.

She got in the van and the other two men from RC's meeting were inside. They looked like Marines, strong faces, masculine builds, short hair, with intense personalities and no smiles on their faces. Becca instinctively knew none of these men were to be messed with, and judging by their lack of facial expression, felt like they were about to go into battle.

"Here." RC put a duffel bag in Becca's lap. "Get dressed."

She unzipped the bag and found within a hot pink bondage dress, white Louboutin six-inch heels in her size, and a white thigh-length fur vest. "You wish."

"Actually, I prefer my women in jeans and tank tops," RC said. "Seriously, I need you to put that on...now."

"What the hell for?" Becca exclaimed.

"Out of everyone in this vehicle, you're the only person those clothes fit."

Becca could tell RC was enjoying bossing her around. She wasn't having any of it. "First thing I'm going to do when we get to the hotel is take a shower."

"We're not going to the hotel."

"ETA ten minutes, Mr. Carter," the driver informed.

"Thank you."

Becca's frustration had already gotten the better of her. "Where are we going, RC?"

"We're on our way to break into the Kremlin. So please stop questioning me and change your clothes."

"Are you insane?" Becca looked at the others in the van and could tell they were already mentally prepared for the mission. "We're going now?"

"You're running out of time, Becca."

RC's hurry-up tone annoyed her. Becca undressed, embarrassed and terrified of where they were heading, and felt completely unprepared. She took off her shirt, revealing her bra for all the men to see. She looked in all the mirrors to see if anyone watched her disrobe. To her comfort, the men of the squad were looking away and to her horror RC kept his eyes peeled on her.

"Are you going to tell me why I have to dress like Svetlana from the street or are you going to keep me guessing?"

"You're the distraction for the Kremlin guards so we can neutralize them."

Becca struggled with the bondage dress in the moving van. She would never admit it out loud, but this was the first time she'd ever worn one. "And what happens if they don't get distracted?"

"You don't have to worry about that." RC smiled. "Believe me."

Becca put on the high heels and felt dizzy from the motion of the van. The stress of what she was about to do didn't help either.

"You do know how to flirt, right?" RC asked to Becca's horror.

In truth, Becca had never flirted before because she was too much of a bookworm. "I really want to punch you in the face right now."

RC pulled out a flask and poured vodka on his hands. "Lean forward and hold up your hair, please."

Becca did as requested. RC gently patted Becca's neck with his wet hands and continued to give her instructions. "You only have to focus on the main objective. Distract both guards. Your clothes and the smell of vodka will do most of the work for you. Smile, bat your eyes, and genuinely ask for help. Believe me, they will fall for the illusion."

The intense fumes from the vodka stung her nose and eyes. She knew that any time she'd smell vodka, she'd think of RC. Becca hated that she really liked RC's hands on her neck. "Where will you be if it all goes south?"

"Not far. We've got you covered."

"Approaching destination," the driver said.

Becca put on the thigh-length fur vest. They had made it this far, and Becca did trust RC in these situations. "This isn't going to keep me warm in this chilly weather."

"You've got this," RC said.

Becca nodded. The van pulled up against the sidewalk and she opened her door to step out. She put one foot outside and RC shoved her out of the car onto the ground. The van drove off quickly.

Becca stood up, pissed, and cursed at the van. She knew she would have bruises from her fall and realized a couple of pedestrians were watching her but had no interest in helping her. She immediately changed the cursing from English to Russian as it dawned on her she was now playing a role and her life depended on it.

13

RC and his Griffin gang had left Becca at the Borovitskaya Tower of the Kremlin. The tower's entrance was about one hundred feet away from her. Problem was, in her heels, it felt like one thousand feet. Becca couldn't help but wonder how professional women worked in shoes like these all night, but she quickly refocused her attention on the task at hand. Distract the guards by seducing them. It was as if RC's voice replayed in her head telling her what to do.

The closer she got to the guards the more nervous she became. She had never been on a date before, let alone seduced anyone. Becca felt completely ridiculous, which didn't add to her confidence at all.

She arrived through the archway and saw two male guards who looked to be in their mid-twenties, one guard at the gate and another in a security booth.

"Do you have a phone?" Becca asked the guard at the gate in Russian. She tried to act desperate. "My boyfriend's a real jerk. He dumped me here and stole my phone. Will you help me?"

The guard from the security booth came over to see what was going on. To her amazement and disgust, RC was right, again. Her clothing was doing the trick. Both men had a predator-like interest in her.

"Where are you from?" one guard asked. "Your Russian is quite impressive for an American."

Becca did her best to focus and not break character. "New York, but I came to Russia when I was fourteen. I live in the Barrikadnaya area and need to get back or my boss will be very angry with me. Can you call a taxi for me?"

One guard stepped toward her and held out his hand. "Identification."

Becca froze. This was it. This was how she was going to get locked in a Russian prison for life. Caught in a lie, dressed as a prostitute, and no identification papers to save her.

"Your identification," the guard demanded, causing Becca to jump.

"All right!" Becca said, "No need to get your uniform wrinkled." She patted her furry vest pretending to look for her ID. She was buying seconds.

She opened her vest revealing the rest of her bondage dress. The guard wasn't fazed and just held his hand out, waiting for Becca.

"There's no ID on me. It's in my purse, which was left in my boyfriend's car. That's why I need to make a call." She could tell the guards didn't trust her. Honestly, she wouldn't have trusted herself either.

"Shift change," the other guard said. "Let them deal with her." He collapsed to the ground.

Becca watched as the guard standing in front of her tried to understand what just happened to his colleague.

"What the hell is this?" The guard grabbed his radio, then fell to the ground before he could call anyone.

Startled, Becca turned around and saw it was RC and his men in Kremlin guard uniforms. Like clockwork, RC's men grabbed the two sleeping guards and hid them out of sight in the booth. RC pressed a button on his cell phone. "Fifteen seconds."

One of RC's men hacked into the security feed and looped all the cameras. RC handed Becca a bag. "Change."

She ran into the booth and quickly changed into her Russian uniform, which, to no surprise, fit her perfectly.

"We can't stay hacked into the video surveillance very long, otherwise our presence will be detected," RC informed them. "Becca, you come with me. We have exactly forty-five seconds to get from this booth to the Secret Tower before my team reactivates the live video surveillance. Are you ready to run?"

"No!" Becca couldn't believe how quickly everything was happening. She tied her boots and absorbed the enormity of her surroundings. Two members of RC's team replaced the guards to maintain the façade of normality.

This was really happening. In just a few moments, once Becca finished tying her bootlaces, she, RC, and the final Griffin of the squad would enter the Kremlin.

"Waiting on you, Becca," RC reminded.

"Shut up." Becca barked more than she realized. The pressure had gotten to her and she didn't need to be nagged. She finished tying her boots and took a few deep breaths.

"Forty-five seconds. Go."

RC, Becca, and the other Griffin raced through the Kremlin entrance. Becca had never seen people run so fast and she found it difficult to keep up. Worse, she really had no idea of how they would get into the Secret Tower; therefore, her life was once again dependent on RC.

Becca realized that RC had chosen a route between the brush and the massive wall itself. It was a good plan. The height of the brush limited outside viewers from seeing them and provided cover for their intrusion.

It was a surprisingly simple plan and could actually work to their benefit, as long as the cameras were looped and they didn't bring attention to themselves.

"Here it is," RC said quietly as they arrived at the Secret Tower's reinforced wooden door.

Becca watched RC rush to pull out his phone and hack into the upgraded security lock on the old door.

"Ten seconds," the other squad member alerted.

Becca looked around to see if anyone had noticed them. Her heart thudded louder than ever before. If one person saw them, they'd be screwed.

A latch clicked and RC quickly opened the door for both Becca and the squad member to enter the Secret Tower. The Griffin went first, Becca dove inside the tower entrance after him, followed by RC, who closed the door behind them and reset the lock.

Becca held her breath waiting for RC to confirm whether they were clear to continue or not. It felt as if she waited for hours when in reality it was mere seconds.

"We're in," RC said quietly.

Becca let out a soft sigh of relief.

"Let's go," RC whispered, not wasting an unnecessary moment.

RC led the way underground into the tunnels. The spiral steps inside the Secret Tower must have been restored at some time for safety even though they still looked and felt ancient. There was a sturdy handrail along both sides of the steep steps.

Kremlin guards' voices echoed throughout the underground tunnels of the tower.

"Keep moving," RC whispered as they descended the staircase until it ended in an abandoned room with a dirt floor covered with small rocks and surrounded by stone walls. RC activated the flashlight on his phone to illuminate the room.

"It's empty. Nothing's here," Becca said. "Why would the map lead us to nothing?"

"Or..." RC did something with his phone.

It looked as if RC's phone was able to X-ray the room and see behind the walls. Becca watched as the flashlight scanned each wall. The light revealed a very strange contraption behind a hidden door in the northwest wall.

"We're in the right place," RC said quietly. "That's a relief."

Becca studied the contraption behind the door. "Looks like some sort of ancient lock system."

"I don't have any technology that will be effective to open the door," RC said. "We'll have to open it the old-fashioned way. Anyone bring a sledgehammer?" he joked.

"That would be the worst thing to try," Becca said, still studying the door. "It looks like it's designed to permanently lock if forced entry is used. It's quite impressive actually."

She pointed to certain stones on the projected X-ray of the door. "If we broke any of these points, mechanisms would lock into place and we'd never be able to break through the door without getting a bulldozer down here or a jackhammer. These locks are made of concrete."

"So which ones do we press?" the Griffin asked.

"And in what order?" Becca added as she thought out loud.

Becca remembered the map from the apartment, and pictured it clearly, as if it were right in front of her.

"RC, shine the flashlight over here." With the help of the X-ray app, she studied certain stones on the wall and on the floor at the base of the door. She found two stones on the floor that had special mechanisms behind them and two stones with the same mechanisms were visible near the top. She remembered a faded sketch of a man on the map with his arms and legs spread out like an X. Becca moved closer to the stone wall with the secret door and placed her feet in front of the two stones on the floor. She reached up to the two above her but they were just out of her reach.

"Damn it." Becca faced RC. "It's designed for a man. I can't reach the top. Give me the phone."

RC and Becca switched places. Becca held the phone up so the projection stayed on the wall for RC to see which stones to place his hands and feet into. "You have to keep your hands and feet touching the stones at the same time or it won't work."

RC placed his hands and feet on the correct stones.

"Now, before you do anything, we have to make sure it's the right sequence otherwise it's locked away for good," Becca said.

"Okay, lady Sherlock. Any ideas what the sequence might be? Hands first, feet first?" RC asked.

"This was designed by a Griffin. You tell me. How does your secret cult like to make locks?"

"First off, we're not a cult…" RC began.

"We would do the unexpected," the Griffin interrupted. "I say feet first then hands. Hands would be the most obvious to use first."

"Can we make a decision quickly? My arms are getting tired," RC said.

Becca nodded. "I agree, feet first…but wait." She continued to ponder the possible combinations in silence.

"Oh, for God's sake," RC sighed. "Hurry up."

Becca muttered to herself. "Left foot then right foot? Right hand then left foot? No, no, too obvious."

"Any day now," RC said. Becca could see sweat trickle down his temples and his arms start to shake.

"Russians read left to right, top to bottom. If the Griffins are fans of doing the unexpected, and the mechanic was Russian, I would make it the opposite. Bottom to top, right to left."

"Here goes nothing," RC said.

Becca bit her lip as she nervously watched RC.

"Right foot," RC said as he pushed the lever back.

A big *CLANK* echoed around the small room and everyone could see through RC's phone scanner the mechanism moved accordingly.

"I think we're okay," Becca said. "Left foot now."

RC pushed the left stone back. *CLANK*. More mechanisms adjusted.

RC pulled the right-hand stone down and then the left-hand stone and stood back as the mechanisms kicked into gear. Dirt and dust fell all over the place, filling up their lungs, as many concrete walls slowly moved out of the way revealing the secret passageway.

14

The light from RC's cell phone wasn't bright enough to illuminate the entire secret passageway. Becca could tell that more concrete walls were still opening along the path by the rumbling sounds that echoed from the distance. A loud thud reverberated throughout, revealing the passageway.

"I think that's it," RC said as he shook out his sore arms. Using his cell phone's flashlight again, they slowly entered through the cloud of dust and dirt that concealed the room.

Becca and the Griffin activated the flashlights on their cell phones to add more light to the dark tunnel. It didn't help much. Becca marveled at the decades-old engineering for the tunnel as she passed each mechanism. She wished she'd had her mechanical engineering degree to understand how this locking system could have been built in the 1930s.

"Clever," she said louder than expected. Becca looked ahead and saw RC's light reveal a strange round shape not too far from them.

"There!" Becca said, full of excitement. She shined her light in the same direction as RC's. "It's the well I'd read about online." She ran to the well as fast as possible.

"Becca, wait!" RC shouted. "You don't know if there are any traps."

Becca ignored RC as she aimed her cell phone's flashlight at the stone well and walked around it multiple times.

"You really need to keep your emotions in check on missions, Becca," RC said with anger as he and the Griffin caught up to her. "You could have been killed or gotten all of us killed."

"I'm sorry. I was overcome with excitement," she replied.

"In this world, think before acting. It'll save your life," RC stated.

"Message received," Becca said sincerely. She knew she'd screwed up, not used to thinking ahead of every move she made. She walked around the well and studied its construction.

"Why was the well filled with concrete?" RC asked while Becca searched each stone.

"There's no recorded information why they decided to build it. This passageway and the well were built-in 1485. The passageway was used as a way to escape in the event of a siege. Sometime in the 1930s the Soviets filled up the well and blocked the exit," Becca replied with a shrug.

"And it's a good place to hide something you don't want to be found," RC said as he got closer to the well. "Let me activate the scanner to speed things up."

"Found it!" Becca said with excitement. "It's the Griffin symbol. Just like on the map." She traced her fingers around a very small etching of a Griffin that was engraved at the bottom left corner of a stone block in the well.

"Move," RC said. He X-rayed the stone. "No booby traps that I can see." He and the Griffin stood on each side of the stone and pressed a specific app on their cell phones.

Becca watched with fascination as they aimed the headphone jack of their phones at the grout around the stone. Lasers pierced through the grout, causing it to crumble. Once the stone was loosened, RC and the Griffin pulled the stone from the well using their fingers.

Becca shined her light into the space left by the removal of the stone and saw what looked like a metal box.

"Give me some light, please." Becca handed her phone to RC, who shined the light into the opening as Becca reached inside with both hands. She felt a metal handle and pulled the box toward her. She struggled a bit as the edges of the box scraped against the sides of the opening but was nonetheless successful in removing the box from its enclosure. She caught the Griffin holding his cell phone as if he was recording her.

"Is that necessary right now? I don't like being on camera." Becca placed the box on top of the well.

"It's policy to record every find," RC said.

Becca took a deep breath as she located the rusted latch on the box.

"Wait," RC ordered. He X-rayed and scanned the box, then said, "Open with care."

Becca placed her fingers on the latch and slowly pulled it up. She felt if she pulled with too much strength the latch would break because the box was so fragile. She gently wiggled the latch to its upright position. With both hands, Becca opened the top of the metal box and peered inside.

An old burgundy cloth made of wool cloaked an oval shape hidden beneath. Becca pinched the cloth and gently unveiled an elephant with the shape of a golden man sitting on top of the armorial bearings of the Danish Royal Family. Becca's eyes widened and her heart beat faster and faster as she continued to remove the cloth from the artifact.

RC brought the cell phone light closer to the box and the Griffin moved in to film the find.

"Look at that," Becca whispered as she gazed at the golden ornamentation and precious stones that were masterfully crafted around a light blue and white enamel egg supported by golden lions at the base.

The Griffin recording the video moved closer to the egg, slowly panning the camera, capturing all the details of the priceless artifact.

"I found it," Becca said quietly as the moment sank in. She couldn't believe it. She had just uncovered the location of a one-hundred-and-twenty-one-year-old artifact. This all started with a silly idea for a thesis. She felt an overwhelming sense of joy mixed with relief flow through her body. She knew she wasn't moving and probably seemed frozen, but she didn't care as she just stared at the Royal Danish Egg in front of her.

"All right." RC's voice broke Becca's moment. "Let's get out of here."

Becca carefully placed the wool cloth back over the egg and gently closed the lid of the box.

"Brotherhood!" the Griffin shouted a warning to Becca and RC. They both turned and saw three men walking toward them with weapons at the ready.

"Get behind the well!" RC grabbed Becca, who grabbed the metal box and they dove behind the well as bullets unloaded violently in their direction. They scrambled to get out of the line of fire.

Becca caught a quick glimpse at the Griffin as his body jerked sporadically from multiple bullet hits before he fell to the ground dead.

Becca immediately cowered behind the stone well. She brought her legs in close to her body and held tightly to the metal box as dust and dirt burst all around her from the continuous fire. She coughed from the fog of dirt.

RC winced as he pressed his body next to Becca's to avoid the gunfire. She saw blood spilling out of a wound in his leg. He had been hit, and it wasn't a scratch. She quickly opened the box and pulled out the Royal Danish Egg.

"Hold your fire or you'll damage it!" she yelled. After a few more gunshots, the Brotherhood ceased firing their weapons as Becca slowly held the egg up above the well for all to see.

"Don't shoot. Idiots!" She put the egg back in the box and made sure the clasp was locked. Becca saw RC holding his left thigh. Blood spread from underneath his hands as he applied pressure. There wasn't anything around to use as a pressure bandage.

"Rebecca?" a deep voice asked with a tone of disbelief.

That voice, that tone, the way her name was said, she'd know that sound anywhere.

It was her father, Edward Lake.

15

"Oh, you've got to be kidding me," Becca said, disgusted. She leaned her back against the stone wall of the well and tried to catch her breath as rage filled her veins. RC winced again from the wound and Becca knew that if she didn't do something quickly, he wasn't going to make it.

She saw the gold decorative rope on the coat of his Russian uniform and tried to rip it off with her hands. No use.

RC shuffled through his pants pocket and pulled out a pocketknife. He handed it to her. She cut the rope and wrapped it tightly around his leg as a tourniquet to slow down the bleeding.

"Out of all the archeologists, businessmen, and historians in the world, I never expected my daughter would be capable of discovering a lost artifact." Edward spoke with such a grateful and calm manner that the hair on her arms stood up.

Becca heard slow clapping from her father as she ripped part of her uniform shirt off and wrapped it around RC's wound. She and RC applied pressure together.

"Come on out and hand it over," her father ordered in a calm voice.

Becca knew there was no other option. If there was any

possibility of getting RC and herself out of this situation alive, she had to play along.

RC spoke quietly between short breaths. "How do you know he won't kill you the moment you stand up?"

"I don't," Becca replied softly. "If you have a better idea, don't keep it to yourself." Another gunshot hit the well near them. Becca covered her head, frightened.

"Hurry up!" her father demanded.

Becca held the box up over her head and slowly rose to her feet. Flashlights shined brightly in her face, limiting her visibility, making it difficult to see the three men. She was able to deduce that her father stood behind two men with guns.

"How long have you been working for the Brotherhood?" She held onto the box tightly, not wanting to let it go.

"Rebecca, did you hit your head? I'm on a hunt. It's as simple as that. I don't know of any Brotherhood."

"He's lying," RC said from behind the well. "They never admit their organization exists."

"Clearly, all the excitement has made you and your friend delusional."

"I would have thought you were a better liar than that, Ed." She knew he hated it when she called him Ed. He was no real father to her, so he didn't deserve the honor of being called Father or Dad.

"How's your mother these days?"

He said it with such grim satisfaction that rage boiled within her soul. She could still see her mother's bruised and swollen face from her recent beating. "You son of a bitch!"

She cautiously moved around the well and saw her father's disgusting smile from the shadows. "If you lay one more finger on her I swear I'll kill you myself."

"Rebecca, please don't waste my time with useless threats. You're an eighteen-year-old girl who's in way over her head and I'm on a schedule."

"So, what's the deal? I give you the egg and the Brotherhood pays you some ridiculous amount for a finder's fee? Then what?" She could tell he wasn't going to answer. "How long have you been working for them anyway? You could at least tell me that since I did all the hard work."

"No one will ever know you and your friend were here. The egg is mine." He made a hand motion and one of his men walked up to Becca and took the metal box out of her hands. She didn't give it up easily, but when she stared down the barrel of his handgun she yielded. The man gave the metal box to Edward, who opened it and took the egg out to admire its magnificence up close.

After a moment, he placed the egg back in the box. "We're done here." Edward immediately turned and headed toward the entrance. The men with guns kept their weapons aimed at Becca as they backed out of the secret room.

"Becca, what's happening?" RC said with a faint voice.

"They're leaving with the egg." She kept her focus on the men, afraid to make any sudden moves. Edward and his men exited the secret room to the chamber beyond and her heart sank when they stopped and faced her. Part of her hoped they would just keep moving and leave them alone. They had the egg anyway, but loose ends still needed to be tied up. No daughter pass here.

"The sequence to close the doors, daughter," Edward commanded.

She was surprised at how not surprised she was that there wasn't a shred of human decency in Edward. She had always suspected he was incapable of human emotion, and part of her had hoped that one day he would prove her wrong, but now it was evident that day would never arrive. He was literally asking her to bury herself alive.

He raised his handgun and pointed it directly at her. "The sequence." His voice echoed throughout the room.

Becca raised her hands defeated. "Left to right, top to bottom."

She heard the other two men press the levers and the door began to move.

"I'm looking forward to celebrating my new find with your mother," Edward taunted.

Becca took a step forward. "I'll kill you," she shouted.

"Rebecca, you'll already be dead. It took me long enough. To get rid of you, that is."

As the door slowly slid shut, a few hinges snapped. The mechanics along the secret room's walls began to shudder and break, causing a domino effect where all the doors juddered open and closed repeatedly.

Becca saw Edward and his men in the distance hurriedly run up the staircase of the tower, heading for safety.

She rushed to RC. "We've gotta go, *now.*" She put his arm around her neck and helped him to his feet. He was heavier than he looked, plus with only one functioning leg and a lot of blood loss, she might as well have been carrying dead weight.

"What did you do?" RC asked weakly, "You gave him the wrong sequence."

"Oh good. You were paying attention." She helped him around the well to the malfunctioning doors.

"Oh hell," RC said. "You're joking, right?"

"I'm not dying down here with you, Reed Alexander Carter. Just follow my lead this time." They watched the random opening and closing of doors blocking their path to safety.

"We're gonna die," RC sighed.

"Shut up, I'm focusing," Becca said as she watched and timed the opening and closing of the first set of doors in their path. In her mind, she calculated what it would take to make it through each set safely.

"You're crazy."

RC was no help.

"On three. One, two, three!" Becca and RC stepped through without getting flattened. RC caught his breath as Becca focused on the timing of the next set of doors. They were opening and closing faster than the first. Becca knew RC was in serious pain and each step would be harder and harder for him to the point where he would fall unconscious at any moment.

The second set of doors slammed closed and opened rapidly. Becca watched, counting to herself for a few moments. "I've got it. Are you ready?"

"No!" RC said. "I'm slowing us down."

"I've calculated that too. We go on every two and four. You got it?"

She watched RC take a couple of deep breaths and muster through his pain. He nodded in agreement.

"Ready," Becca said. "Now!" They stepped together on the proper count, making it through to the third set of pounding doors. "This is the last set of moving doors we have to get through. The one after is locked open in place, but it's a small opening and we'll have to squeeze through one at a time. So, we make this, and then it gets easier. Got it?"

RC sank to the floor out of breath.

"Come on. We're halfway there. Stay with me, RC."

"I need a second," he said.

"We don't have a second, come on!" Becca helped him back up to his feet and she timed the sequencing of the fastest set of doors. "We can't make this one together."

"What does that mean?" RC asked.

"It's too fast for both of us to go at the same time. We have to cross one at a time."

The doors slammed repeatedly in front of them. "You go first," Becca said as she maneuvered herself behind RC. "I'll push you through."

He nodded his understanding.

Becca watched the doors slam in front of them. She took a deep breath. "Take a half step forward." RC did as instructed. "Ready? Now!" She shoved RC through the doors and he fell to the ground. He did make it through. Becca waited for her turn to clear the doors and leaped through. The door smashed together behind her, ripping part of her pant leg.

Becca once again helped a rapidly fading RC to his feet and made him go sideways through the small opening between the non-slamming doors. She pushed him through and continued to praise him for every step, trying to keep him alert, then she followed him.

Together they exited the secret room into the basement of the Secret Tower.

"We made it!" Becca exhaled her fear.

The walls of the basement began to rumble and crack as rubble fell from the ceiling. Becca looked up.

"It's caving in, *move!*" Becca shoved RC forward and up the staircase, helping him hop each step. She stayed focused on RC even though she could hear the stones and walls collapsing behind her.

"Keep going, you've got this." She didn't care how ridiculous she sounded supporting him. She would do whatever it took to get both of them to safety.

RC hopped the next stone step and collapsed forward, completely unconscious.

"No, no, no, RC!" Becca put her arms beneath his armpits and dragged him up the steps. Sweat poured down her temples as adrenaline coursed through her body, giving her the strength, she needed to pull him up the winding staircase. She got to the main door of the tower and shoved it open, then sprinted backward as fast as she could, dragging RC away from the collapsing tower. She felt her chest tighten as she watched the secret tower of the Kremlin implode in front of her. She tripped backward, dropping RC, and quickly covered him with her body as the last of the debris fell near them.

Dirt and dust clouds surrounded them. Becca's legs throbbed. The scrapes on her arms stung and ached, and she could barely breathe. She rested her head on RC's chest and passed out to the sound of oncoming sirens.

16

Becca slowly came to. She didn't know where she was. Her blurry vision took longer than normal to adjust to her surroundings. She was in a room, a bedroom, and no lights were on. She didn't know how she got there. The darkness of the room told her it was night, so she'd been there for hours. Her vision finally focused and she could tell she was in a small room that didn't have much, just a bed, one dresser, and one nightstand. On the nightstand was a jug of water and a cup.

She heard male voices outside her bedroom door and could tell they were still in Russia from the dialect. Unfortunately, Becca didn't recognize any of the voices and she couldn't fully hear what was being said.

The bedroom door opened and let in blaring bright light, completely silhouetting the person entering. Fear overcame Becca and she hurriedly searched for something to use as a weapon. She jolted with pain, letting out a louder cry than she expected. She looked down and saw that she had bandages all over her body, big and small.

"Oh good, you're awake," the woman's voice said from the doorway as she flipped on the light switch in the room.

Becca didn't believe her eyes. "Mom?"

Standing before Becca was her bruised and beaten mother. Tears of relief formed at seeing her mother in person. They came so rapidly that she didn't realize how afraid she had been until she let out her tears. Vivian rushed to Becca's bedside and hugged her tightly.

"I'm so relieved you're safe," her mother said. "Try not to move quickly. You're okay. You just have a few bumps and bruises. No serious injuries."

Becca spoke through her tears. "What's going on? How are you here? Where are we? I'm so happy to see you."

"I'm happy to see you too, honey." They embraced each other tightly. "You're in a safe house."

The last few hours all rushed back to Becca like a brick to the head. Losing the egg to her father, the collapse of the secret tower, RC's injury, and passing out after she barely escaped. One piece of the puzzle didn't fit. How did her mother know?

Becca immediately noticed something different about her mother. She seemed, for lack of a better term, more confident than she had remembered. The way she spoke to Becca, the way she comforted her, and even the way she looked at her. It was almost as if she was talking to a different mother. She didn't seem like a weak pushover but instead, she seemed better, stronger.

Becca pulled away from Vivian cautiously. "How do I know I'm talking to my real mother?" Becca asked.

"Becca, are you serious?" Vivian said, surprised.

Becca gained control of her tears and looked dead serious at Vivian. "What's the password?" she asked.

Becca and her mother had a pact that if something dangerous ever happened to either of them and a stranger they didn't recognize offered help as a friend, to ask them the password. Only true friends of her and her mother knew the correct password. If the woman Becca stared at was indeed her mother, this would be an easy test to pass.

Becca waited for an answer, concerned that the Brotherhood of the Fox might have done something to her mother.

"If you spell evil backward, you get the word live. To deal with evil is to live life," Vivian said.

Becca sighed with relief. "It really is you." She hugged her mother again tightly but winced as she forgot that she was bruised all over her body.

"Careful, Becca. Don't move so suddenly." Vivian helped Becca lean back onto her pillow. "You need to let your muscles heal. You overworked them. Dragging RC's heavy body away from falling debris with no training will do that."

"Wait. How do you know about that?"

"I was briefed on my way over from the States. Mason Carter pulled me in the moment they received the distress signal from RC's phone."

"Mason Carter?" Becca exclaimed. "How do you know Mason Carter?"

"There was a team of Griffins just outside the tower watching it collapse. You got to the surface just in time, then passed out moments before they were able to extract you."

Becca couldn't believe it. "You're...like RC? You're a Griffin?"

Vivian nodded, confirming Becca's suspicion. It didn't make any sense to her. Her mother couldn't be a member of the League of Griffins. She just didn't seem capable of being one of them.

"No. That's not possible." Becca tried to connect the dots in her mind. "I'm so confused."

"Just relax, Becca. Mason Carter has cleared me to loop you in." Vivian grabbed Becca's hand and held it firmly. "The information I'm about to tell you is highly classified and before you say anything, know that I love you very much."

Becca waited impatiently. "Okay."

"Nineteen years ago, I was assigned to go undercover and seduce your father. For years the Griffins had been gathering information to narrow down the current leaders of the Brotherhood all over the world. We lost a lot of men and women in the process of acquiring the correct intelligence."

It was very strange to hear her mother speak so precisely. It was almost uncanny for Becca, but she let her mother continue without interruption.

"Once the information was solid enough to suspect Edward Lake as a possible member of the Brotherhood, I was tasked with getting close to him to confirm the intelligence."

"Why you?" Becca interrupted.

"I matched the profile that had been built about your father. I was the right height, eye color, natural hair color, everything. Your father is an extremely clever man and very suspicious of anyone he meets. He had suspected other women in the past were sent to spy on him and they, sadly, are not with us anymore."

"How did you not get caught?"

"Mason and I developed a plan, pinpointing where your father would be at an exact moment in time. Our research had shown that your father's ultimate vulnerability was after he had made a discovery during an archeological dig. His success was my way into his favor. I couldn't approach him at all. He had to come to me of his own free will."

"You're kidding. You were assigned and willingly let that monster do whatever he wanted to do to you?"

"It was the only way to throw him off the scent. Mason helped me set up the proper backstory, as we knew Edward would check into my background the following day if I had survived my first night with him. I passed his test and made him believe that I enjoyed his abusive nature. That was the only way I could stay in his circle and the only way I survived."

Becca quickly found herself seeing the true depth of her mother. She wasn't a weakling or a woman who would just let any man step all over her. She was playing a part. The most difficult part any woman could play. Becca couldn't imagine having to do what her mother did to survive.

"When I became pregnant and found out you were going to be a girl, Edward wanted an abortion."

"I know. He told me multiple times growing up. That's not something you forget."

Vivian continued. "You don't know why." Vivian grabbed the jug of water on the nightstand and poured some into a cup for Becca to drink.

"Edward never told me this, but the Griffins discovered that leaders of the Brotherhood are only allowed to have sons to continue the legacy. If word got out that he had a girl, he would've lost his rank and been terminated to preserve the purity of the Brotherhood leadership."

"How am I still alive if he's not allowed to have a daughter?" One of the most loving smiles she'd ever seen appeared on her mother's face.

"Having you was a blessing in disguise," Vivian said. "It gave me leverage over Edward. I told him that if he harmed you in any way, I would never let him touch me again, he'd have to kill me."

"You made yourself invaluable to him."

"All men have their vices, and Edward Lake's is dominance over me," Vivian said.

This newfound knowledge carried more weight than expected and Becca's world once again had been turned upside down.

"So all those times I never understood why you let him abuse you, you did it to keep me alive and continue to spy on him."

"When I told you he loved me in his own way, it was true. He loved using me for his personal needs, so I made sure that I'd be the only one that he'd want to continue to use to satisfy him."

Becca felt a little sick and drank some water. "I thought you were so blinded by a ridiculous love that you'd never see the light of day."

"I never loved your father," Vivian said with all the strength in the world. "He was a target and nothing more."

Becca wished she had known, but immediately understood why

she wasn't told. "I'm sorry for thinking any less of you." Becca gave her mother another hug.

"I wouldn't have been doing a good job if you didn't think that. It wasn't easy to keep your father's trust, but for nineteen years I have been secretly feeding information to the Griffins about your father's whereabouts and how he has risen up the ranks of the Brotherhood." Vivian separated from Becca and looked her right in the eyes, strictly business. "But now, thanks to your adventure at the Kremlin, I'm also a target."

17

A man entered the bedroom, interrupting Becca and Vivian. He was tall, bald, and had a very muscular physique. His presence was incredibly intimidating and very Russian. There was no doubt in Becca's mind he was someone you didn't want to mess with. He probably had at least three firearms underneath his trench coat.

"Boss wants you," the man said to Vivian with a deep Russian accent. He didn't pay any real attention to Becca, as his demeanor read strictly business.

"Give me a minute," Vivian replied.

The man returned to the living room, shutting the door behind him. Becca instinctively grabbed her mother's arm as Vivian got up from the bed.

"Becca," Vivian said calmly, "you're safe. Everyone here is a member of the Griffins. The Brotherhood has no idea where we are."

Becca still held on to her mother. "Is RC okay?"

"The doctor is with him in the other room," she said. "He'll recover in time. You saved his life."

Becca sighed, relieved that RC was still alive.

"There's food in the kitchen when you're feeling up to it. And if you want to check in on RC, he's in the room across from the living room."

"Yes, I'd like to see him."

Becca slowly got up from the bed with help from her mother. It wasn't easy for her as every time she moved her legs it felt as if she was moving one-hundred-pound weights. Her entire body ached from exhaustion as she entered the living room.

The safe house was pretty basic. Kitchen with an island. One couch and two chairs surrounded a coffee table next to an unused fireplace in the small living room. The rooms smelled like coffee, reminding her it'd been hours since she'd eaten anything.

The house was a little bit bigger than Becca had originally thought. It had three bedrooms. To no surprise, RC was in the master bedroom. The door was open and she could see him lying in bed asleep while the doctor checked a hanging pouch of blood that RC was hooked up to. She watched her mother enter the other bedroom opposite hers and close the door. Clearly, her mother's meeting was private.

Becca bypassed the kitchen and entered RC's room. He seemed peaceful as he slept. She'd never tell him to his face, but he was cute to watch sleep. Too bad he was such a hothead when he was awake.

The doctor acknowledged Becca with a little head nod and returned his attention to his notes. Becca saw the symbol of a Griffin feather on the doctor's wrist. One day she was going to ask RC what the different tattoos meant.

"He wouldn't have made it if we were five minutes later," the doctor said without looking up from his notes. "He owes you, big time. Well done."

Becca smiled, grateful for the compliment. She slowly moved to RC's side, and the doctor set up a chair for Becca to sit in. "How long will it take for him to be back to his usual self?"

"About a week at this rate. We've developed substantial ways to speed up the recovery process, but sometimes there's no better cure than good old-fashioned rest. Same goes for you."

Becca looked at RC as he lay motionless in the bed. "I just want to spend a little time with him, if that's all right."

"Of course." The doctor placed his clipboard on the dresser and smiled at Becca. "I'll leave you two alone for a bit." He exited the room and shut the door behind him.

"You hear that?" Becca asked quietly. "You owe me. Doctor's orders." She smiled at her own joke as she continued to watch RC rest.

"To have the great Reed Alexander Carter owe me. Wow." She thought about it for a second. "I could probably get anything I've ever wanted now." She leaned closer to him on the bed. "Imagine how jealous all the women of the world would be if they knew. I'd probably be the most hated girl on social media." Becca sat back in the chair and continued her silly little taunt of RC. "I'm not going to lie. I do feel a little awesome, aside from the pain all over my body. Luckily, pain is temporary. We certainly cut it close there, didn't we? Any chance we could avoid that next time?"

She felt safer around RC, especially after what they both had been through and she would never admit it out loud to him, but she hated seeing him in his current state. It made her feel completely vulnerable to any attack.

"Don't get me wrong. I don't mind the adventure. Finding the clues, putting the big puzzle together. But the violence. I don't think I'll ever get used to that." She grabbed his hand in hers. "Honestly, I don't know if I can survive this without you. So, will you heal quickly? Please?"

Becca hoped RC would answer her, but none came. After a few moments, she let go of his hand, got up from the chair, and exited the room, quietly closing the door behind her.

The kitchen had plenty of food. There were too many choices. She was so hungry, it was overwhelming for her to make a decision. She ultimately settled for a banana, peanut butter, and chocolate pudding. Not necessarily the best choices, but after almost being crushed by a tower, she felt she deserved something simple.

She heard her mother's voice get louder from the room where the meeting was taking place. It didn't sound like it was going well. Becca took a few steps closer to the closed door trying to understand what they said, but what she could hear didn't make any sense. She decided to leave it alone for the time being and would ask her mother when the opportunity arose.

Becca returned to her room with her snacks and saw her phone on the nightstand next to the water jug. With a moan, she slowly sat back down on the bed and pulled her feet up, one leg at a time. Becca grabbed her phone and saw she had forty missed texts and emails from Barry. One read, "Saw what happened at the Kremlin on TV. U ok?"– Barry. Another read, "Becca, I'm freakin' out here. Get back to me so I know ur alive." – Barry.

Becca saw the remainder of texts and emails all had the same message of concern. She typed in her reply. I'm alive. It's not safe to text at the moment. She pressed send but the text didn't go through. She pressed send again and nothing.

"What the hell?" Becca sighed.

Hello Rebecca Hunter Lake, her phone's automated voice said, startling her. *This is DIANA. May I be of assistance?*

"Umm." Becca knew DIANA was the Griffins' A.I. that she'd seen back in Mason's office, but wasn't expecting it on her phone. "I'm trying to text my friend Barry and the message won't go through."

That's because your phone is not secure, DIANA replied. *You cannot send any emails, texts, or make any phone calls until your phone has been secured. Your phone is currently restricted to only using certain authorized game apps, and to search the Internet for monitored browsing pleasure.*

Becca sighed, a little frustrated at being restricted even if she did understand the importance. "How do I secure my phone calls?"

You must enter the correct security code or an authorized fingerprint on the touch screen.

Well, that was just great. Becca didn't know who locked her

phone while she was passed out. It could've been her mother or one of the big Griffin guys. She had no idea what the security code would be if the Griffin men had restricted it, but if her mother had locked the phone there could be a few options.

"What's the password?" Becca asked herself. She typed in the numerical numbers 5, 4, 8, 3. "L-I-V-E," she said out loud.

Phone restrictions lifted, DIANA said. *Your phone is now secure.*

"Ha!" Becca smiled at her own cleverness. She clicked on Barry's phone number. Five icons appeared. Text, Call, Facetime, Email, and the other one she didn't recognize. It was the image of a hand with the palm facing up. She pressed the button.

Calling Barry, hologram mode, DIANA said.

The phone screen projected a three-dimensional video hologram in the middle of her bedroom. Just like the hologram she saw back in Mason's office. Barry appeared as a floating three-dimensional image.

"Becca?" The hologram flickered. "Becca, you there?"

"Yes. I'm here. Can you hear me?" Becca could tell that Barry was in his room as safe as ever.

"What the hell has been going on? I was worried sick about you."

"It's…complicated," Becca replied. "I can't tell you anything other than I'm okay."

"Oh, you gotta give me more than that," he exclaimed. "I can see you're pretty banged up. You were at the Kremlin, weren't you?"

Becca hadn't realized how difficult this conversation with her best friend would be. She didn't blame him for being worried and frustrated. If she were in his position, she would feel the same way.

"Barry, you can hate me all you want, but I really can't tell you anything. It's not safe for you or me."

"Let me help," he begged. "I'm going crazy not knowing what's going on. Plus, everything is so boring without you hanging around putting your Fabergé puzzle pieces together."

"That's not smart, Barry," Becca stayed calm, mainly because she didn't have the energy to argue with him. Plus, she knew the best way to reason with him was to just level with him. "You're too important to me and I don't want anything bad to happen to you. I'm in way over my head here and I have no idea how long it will take for me to get out of this."

"So, you *were* at the Kremlin," he clarified.

The stunned look on his face informed Becca of what he was going to say next.

"You found it, didn't you?" Barry said. "Holy shit!"

Becca attempted to bring his excitement back to ground level. "Barry, I can't say anything. The less you know the better."

It was as if he didn't hear her at all. Barry just unloaded with question after question about the egg, where it was in the Kremlin, how heavy it was, and how she had found it. But Becca didn't confirm anything with him. She knew he wasn't mad because she'd always been able to read his facial expressions and interpret his silences.

"I really hate that you know me so well sometimes," Becca sighed.

"Well, congratulations on your first find," he said.

They both laughed and Becca grabbed her side as laughing added to her pain.

"Do you have any idea when you'll be back?" Barry asked.

Becca shook her head, completely uncertain if she was going to make it back at all.

"Hey...hey, look at me, Becca," Barry said. "You need to promise me you'll come back. No matter how difficult your situation may get. Promise me you'll get back here."

Becca desperately wanted to make that promise to Barry. Nothing would make her happier than to know she'd be returning unharmed. "You know I can't make that kind of promise, Barry. There are too many factors that are unaccounted for." She couldn't explain it to him, but she had a gut feeling that nothing would ever be the same.

"I don't care about the factors," Barry protested. "It's a reassurance thing. Promise me."

Becca crossed her fingers out of sight of the hologram. "I promise."

18

A week had gone by, and it was the slowest week ever. Becca felt like she was back in high school waiting for the bell to ring so she could leave, but time just seemed to drone on. Being kept in the dark didn't make things any better either. Her mother had countless private meetings with the other Griffin members staying in the safe house. No doubt they were devising some plan to retrieve the Royal Danish Egg from her father, but the exact game plan was still a mystery. The only thing that battled Becca's cabin fever was her decision to try to piece together as much information about the goings-on in the safe house as she could.

RC had slowly regained consciousness. It was strange because he was nice at first, but as the days went by and he regained his strength, he returned to being his normal cocky self. Becca wondered if the drugs had made RC nice or if somewhere beneath that attitude was a genuinely nice person. She pictured herself on a first date with RC, but it didn't last five minutes before laughter interrupted her thought. The two of them on a coffee date or holding hands at the movie theater just seemed too weird and so not RC.

"What's so funny?" RC startled her as he limped up to the island in the kitchen.

"Nothing," Becca answered as she returned to making herself a peanut butter sandwich.

"You have a weird look on your face," RC persisted. "I can tell it's not nothing."

"How's the leg?" Becca changed the subject. She knew RC wasn't going to let it go, but to her surprise, he respected the deviation.

"Getting stronger every day. There'll be a scar for sure. Not sure how that will affect the mood in the bedroom with the ladies."

That comment completely deflated Becca's enjoyment of this conversation. She didn't need to know, or want to know, about RC's female exploits.

"So, what do you have?" he asked.

Becca held up her peanut butter sandwich.

"Not the sandwich, dork." He smirked. "Information. I know you've been casing the place, dying to know what's going on. What have you found out?"

"Aside from the fact that my mother has secretly been a member of the League of Griffins for twenty years and that my father is enemy number one, not a whole lot." Becca took a bite of her sandwich, frustrated.

"Do better," he said.

"Do better? What does that even mean?" Becca snapped unexpectedly.

"Shhh." RC held his finger to his lips, looking around to make sure they didn't attract attention from the Griffin meeting going on in the other room. "I get that you're pissed, Becca, and you should be angry. I am too. But you have to keep your head about you. This is the time we need to focus."

"But I have no idea what to do. I don't know where to start. What does the Brotherhood plan to do with the egg now that they have it?"

"I don't know. Most of the time they use the artifacts they

acquire to buy weapons, armies, fund terrorism, you name it. But this is different."

"What do you mean it's different? Selling the egg to fund terrorism and ensure another ten years of life for the Brotherhood sounds like a pretty solid plan for them."

"First of all, the Brotherhood doesn't need any money. They've had centuries to accumulate billions of dollars. Secondly, I've never heard of a leader of the Brotherhood in the field on any find. No matter how big or famous the missing artifact was. Usually, they get their minions to find it for them and stay in the shadows. Your father was there in the Secret Tower, in person. That means something. There's something more with the egg. Some other importance."

The door to the meeting room opened and Vivian and the Griffins came into the living room.

"We've been activated," Vivian said. "We have one hour to clear the safe house."

"What's the op?" RC asked.

"I said *we've* been activated," Vivian clarified, "Not you and Becca."

"What?" Becca stared at her mother, confused.

"Mason's orders. I'm to take this team and retrieve the egg from Edward Lake. You two will be taken to the airport and put on a plane back to New York."

"This is ridiculous!" RC shouted.

"You're benched," Vivian scolded, shutting RC up.

Becca was honestly surprised at how her mother had clear control of the room. Her authority was almost scary. Plus, Becca had never seen RC be put in his place. Not even by his father.

"You're in no condition to continue," Vivian told RC. "Edward has resurfaced and if we lose him now, we lose him for good. Mason has given us his orders."

"We can help you." Becca attempted to reason with her mother, but Vivian wasn't having any of it.

"Becca, you and RC have done plenty. You found the Royal Danish Egg and helped us locate one of the leaders of the Brotherhood. You've both done enough. It's our turn to take it from here. These men will help you both pack. End of discussion."

The Griffins immediately began clearing out the place. It was spooky how precise and efficient they were at removing any trace of their presence including food, bedsheets, and dust. Within twenty minutes the place looked like no one had ever been there.

As they exited the safe house, the Griffins carried the suitcases for RC and Becca to the street where two cars waited for them. RC and Becca were directed to the first car. RC climbed in. Becca stayed outside. The Griffin men placed the luggage in the trunk and then got in the second car.

"I want to stay with you," Becca said to her mother.

"No, Becca. It's too dangerous and you're not trained to be in the field. Honestly, it's amazing you've lasted this long. With RC benched, you're just another innocent bystander the Brotherhood won't think twice about killing. I wouldn't be able to live with myself if something happened to you."

"I can still help. I don't have to be in the field," Becca pleaded.

"Becca. Stop. The answer is no. I'm about to go into the lion's den. I have to focus, and having you with me is just another distraction. Plus, if your father sends men or assassins after you, he can use you as leverage over me, or worse." Vivian gave Becca a strong, tight hug. "I need you safe and out of harm's way. Mason has everything taken care of. Now get in the car."

Becca looked into her mother's eyes and saw fire combined with a fierce strength. Her mother was in control of her emotions and knew exactly what she was doing.

Becca nodded, surrendering her desire to change her mother's mind, knowing it to be futile. "Get that bastard," she said coldly. "Make him pay for all the pain he caused you and me."

Vivian had no response on her face. Becca climbed into the front car and sat next to RC. Vivian closed the door behind her. The driver turned over the engine and the car pulled away from the sidewalk. Becca watched her mother get smaller in the distance as she and her men moved into their car.

"This is wrong." RC's frustration didn't go unnoticed. "It's our responsibility to get the egg back. They can't possibly know what they're getting into."

Becca sat back in her seat and faced the front. "It sounds like you're upset that you won't get credit for the find."

"Don't be ridiculous. I could care less about who gets credit for the find as long as it's credited to the Griffins. If anyone should get the credit, it should be you." RC drank water from a bottle that was on the armrest between him and Becca. "What bothers me is that I don't get to pay your father and those foxes back for shooting me in the leg."

"I didn't take you for the revenge type," Becca said.

"Getting shot really changes you," RC replied with a cold tone.

"I hope to never find out."

The car arrived at the airport and pulled up next to another G700 private plane. The driver got out of the car and grabbed their luggage. Becca and RC exited the car and followed the driver onto the plane.

"What about the car?" Becca asked. She noticed there wasn't anyone around. "Do we just leave it here?"

RC went up to the bar and grabbed a water bottle. The driver placed Becca and RC's luggage in the overhead bin.

RC poured cups of water for Becca, himself, and their driver. "Someone will get it ten minutes after we take off. Usually, we have people waiting for us on-site, but with this last-minute change, the priority is stopping the Brotherhood and we take second place on the important list." He handed a cup of water to the driver.

"Thank you, sir." The driver took a sip, then downed the entire thing.

"Don't mention it," RC said.

Becca felt the rage radiating off RC. His body hummed with

fury. It was very clear he didn't like being limited in what he could do and where he could go. It worried Becca. RC was pretty much a loose cannon in the field. Call him a free spirit. Caging someone like him never had the desired effect one would hope. Usually, they lashed out at some point. Almost like a dog that hated being put in the crate.

"May I get anything else for you before we depart?" the driver asked.

Becca started to speak, but RC interrupted.

"No. Just take your seat so we can get out of this country." RC handed a cup of water to Becca and sat across from her. "Let's get this show on the road," he yelled to the pilot.

The plane's engines wound up and the stair door closed.

Becca looked out the window as the engines warmed up. She went to take a drink of water.

"Don't drink that," RC said.

Becca looked at RC, who was staring at the driver completely passed out in his seat. "Oh my God."

RC stood up and checked the driver's pulse. He took Becca's drink from her and tossed it into the sink by the bar.

"What happened?" Becca asked with alarm. "Who put something in the water?"

RC returned from the galley. "I did. Gave him one of my sleeping pills. They're pretty powerful. He'll be out for a few hours. Probably won't come to until he's halfway to New York."

"What do you mean?" Becca watched RC head to the controls for the stairway door.

"We're not going back to New York," he said.

"We've been ordered to," Becca protested.

"Do you always do what you're told?" He looked at Becca with a last-chance vibe. "You can go back if you want, but I'm going to retrieve the egg. Now, are you coming or not?"

It was a no-brainer. She wasn't going anywhere without RC and she didn't care how much trouble she'd be in. "I'm with you."

RC opened the door. He motioned for Becca to go first. She rushed down the stairs.

"Run to the car," RC said quietly.

Becca and RC raced to the car. No surprise, RC took the driver's seat, and Becca got in the passenger seat. She turned to glance at the plane and saw the co-pilot stop on the stairs and look at them, confused.

RC found the keys in the armrest and started the engine. "The pilot has most likely already called it in to headquarters." RC rapidly pressed buttons on the touch screen in the car.

"Let's go, RC," Becca said anxiously. "The co-pilot's coming after us." She watched as his feet ate up the ground under him. "We're not going to make it out of here at this rate."

RC floored the gas pedal. "This isn't the first time ditching my father's bodyguards, Becca."

As they drove away, his fingers flew over the touchpad on the screen in the car. Becca watched him tap an app called Tracking.

"This will deactivate the vehicle's tracking device and buy us some time." As they raced to the gate at the perimeter of the airport, men rushed to close it and keep them inside the airport grounds. The car raced out of the airport just in time, before anyone could stop them. Even though she knew she was in serious trouble, deep down in her heart, going back was the right thing to do.

19

The car zoomed along the highway. RC wasn't paying any attention to the rules of the road. Becca braced herself multiple times as they came close to getting into accidents.

"Where are we going?" she asked, trying to hide the panic in her voice as they changed lanes, narrowly clipping the front bumper of another car as they passed.

"We need to find a place to lay low, to think," RC replied without taking his eyes off the road. It was clear to Becca that RC was in complete control of his mission, but she wasn't used to his reckless driving, nor did she ever want to get used to it.

"Where's a good place to start?" Becca asked. "My mom didn't tell me anything and I didn't hear much in the safe house while you were recovering."

"We need to work on your spying skills," RC said.

Becca decided to take that as a compliment. "I'm not sure what you were doing, but I picked up a few things," RC began. "They've pinpointed your father's location about five hours from here in the mountains."

"How the hell did you figure that out?" Becca couldn't see how

RC could've uncovered any more information than she had. He was barely conscious half the time.

"I used my eyes," he said bluntly. "Did you notice how your mother and the others were dressed when we left the safe house?"

"Umm. No. I was too caught up in the change of plan," Becca said.

"Well, you need to start putting your emotions in check. You can learn a lot from just observing."

Becca didn't like being told to control her emotions. Her first instinct was to be offended, but she quickly realized RC wasn't trying to be cruel, he was teaching her a lesson.

"Think back to when we were leaving."

As RC instructed, Becca saw the layout of the safe house in her mind. "What kind of shoes was everyone wearing?"

Becca thought about it for a quick second and then saw what they wore clearly in her mind. "Combat boots."

"Correct," he said. "Why does someone wear combat boots?"

"Unless you have a serious taste for military fashions, you're going into battle or on a hike. But it's still a big if. That could just be protocol for going on a mission."

"What kind of jackets?" RC asked.

Becca's photographic memory served her well. "Cargo jackets. I don't know the brand. All the pockets were full. Most likely carrying ammunition," she said.

"Good," RC said as they passed more cars on the highway. "Tell me about the cargo bags everyone loaded into the car your mother got into."

"All the bags were full," Becca responded, explaining every detail she saw in her mind. "Some were lighter than others. Maybe carrying a change of clothes."

"And the heavier bags?" RC added.

"Rifles, most likely. But I'm not entirely sure what that means," Becca said.

"Rifles. You're sure about that. Not submachine guns?"

"It could be," Becca replied, not sure about the differences between guns. She had never touched a gun, let alone fired one. She didn't like them. Her knowledge of guns was limited to what she had seen on TV or read in a novel somewhere.

"Griffins rarely use semi-automatic guns. We usually carry silenced handguns for most operations. That allows for quick unnoticed escapes. It's easier to blend into crowds. The only reason to carry heavy weaponry is if we expect to be going into a heavily armed area that's outside," RC explained. "The cargo jackets are hunting jackets," he said calmly. "You see hunters wearing those all the time outdoors. We would wear a vest if it was indoors."

"You're thinking they're in a forest," Becca chimed in.

"The nearest forest is five hours away." RC's knuckles showed white while he gripped the steering wheel.

"How do you plan to find them?" Becca asked.

"I've already activated the squad's tracking device. We need to piggyback the feed. That way we can catch up unnoticed."

"How do we do that?" Becca asked, completely at a loss.

"I'm not sure yet," RC said. "We need outside help. We can't use DIANA, the Griffins constantly monitor her and see every transmission in and out. That helps my father keep track of everyone. If we use her the Griffins will know where we are."

"What if my mother needs help?" Becca asked, worried. The Griffins with her mother appeared more than capable of handling themselves, but she couldn't help but wonder if they were enough for whatever her father had planned for them. "What if they're walking into a trap?"

"The only way to find out is to get there," RC said. He turned the wheel and took a route that led into a tunnel. There wasn't much traffic in the tunnel going in either direction.

"Follow my lead," RC said.

Suddenly RC jerked the car into the opposing lanes and pulled the emergency brake. Becca saw one oncoming car and screamed. Their car skidded to a stop, blocking the oncoming car.

RC got out of the car. "Come on, Becca," he said as he hurried to the other car and grabbed the driver out of his vehicle.

Terrified and confused, Becca followed RC and realized what he was doing. Aside from the obvious carjacking, they were swapping vehicles to cover their tracks. Becca hopped in the passenger side as RC tossed the keys they had been using to the driver. As they drove away in his car, Becca watched the driver grab the keys out of the air and get in their previous car.

"He got a better deal in the long run," RC said as they exited the tunnel. "We probably bought ourselves an extra hour."

"You know, I would prefer it if you would give me a heads up the next time you plan on carjacking someone."

"And miss the surprised look on your face? Not a chance," RC said, smiling.

He was serious and making fun of her inexperience at the same time.

"It's not funny, RC. Let me help. I can only help if I know what the plan is. Last-minute decisions like that freak me out."

"Sometimes last-minute decisions are what keep you alive and on your feet. Like when you stole the cigarette case when we first met."

He was right. She wanted to protest the difference between her decision to steal the case compared to his decision to steal a citizen's car, but she knew she'd lose the argument. Besides, they would've never found the egg if Becca hadn't stolen the case in the first place. Also, they wouldn't be in this mess if she hadn't.

"You can plan to the end of time, Becca," RC said. "But always be open to last-minute changes in the world. If you aren't open, you won't last. Remember that."

Hours went by and RC's driving became more relaxed as they got nearer to the tree-lined mountains. The scent of pine and fresh air lifted her spirits a little.

RC had taught Becca how to use her Griffin phone after telling her how to bypass almost all the restrictions. Usually, these were passcodes given once a member had completed a certain number of tasks for the League of Griffins. But since their phones were the only computers they had at their disposal, it was best to be able to use them to their fullest potential. RC's phone did the same stuff as Becca's, but she needed to get used to using her own equipment.

She learned certain protocols to call for help from the Griffins. How to pinpoint the location of a target, how to piggyback through the Internet to find cyber trails of individuals, how to bypass all security and firewalls. It was fascinating and scary. Something Becca knew Barry would love to know.

"That's it!" she shouted louder than expected. "Barry."

"Who?" RC said.

"We can use my friend Barry to locate everyone. He's a genius with computers."

"That kid from the restaurant I saw you talking with?"

"Yes," Becca said. "Unless you have a better option?"

"Unfortunately, I don't. It's going to be dark soon and nearly impossible to find anyone without giving our location away first."

"Barry will help us. He's always been there for me."

"This isn't for dating advice or schoolwork," RC reminded. "Can you trust him?"

Becca didn't even have to think about it. "I've known Barry since we were eight years old. I trust him with my life."

"Then call him, so we can find your mother." Becca secured her phone's signal and pressed the hologram button, calling Barry.

20

"This is crazy awesome." The hologram of Barry was ecstatic. "I honestly feel slightly guilty seeing all of this. Slightly."

"It's just this one time, Barry," Becca said from the passenger seat. She knew bringing Barry on board was a huge risk and that RC wasn't happy having to share any secrets about the League of Griffins with him.

RC didn't tell Barry too much information. It was impressive, and Barry didn't press certain questions too far. Only when he absolutely needed the most vital information did RC instruct him.

Becca watched the flickering hologram of Barry as he worked his magic on his multiple keyboards. For a second Barry's happiness made Becca forget she was heading into a possible war zone with RC in the driver's seat. It was good seeing Barry do what he did best.

"This is a bad idea," RC said, keeping his eyes on the road.

"We can trust Barry, RC. Besides we don't have any better options," Becca insisted.

"Seeing how joyful he is, worries me," RC muttered. "It's like handing nuclear codes to an infant."

"A really super-smart infant," Barry's hologram corrected as he continued to type on his keyboard.

It was getting darker and there wasn't a single car in sight on the road. Becca thought if she wanted to find a secret society, or a cult of murdering lunatics, this would be the perfect place for them to hide. Miles and miles of forest were ahead of them. It was like searching for a needle in a haystack. No one would survive on their own without protection or proper planning, which she admitted to herself, they didn't have.

"Sweet! I'm in the security system of your mom's car." Barry's voice bleeped in and out. "Holy wow." Barry zoned out for a second.

"Barry, what is it? Hello? Barry." Becca held her phone up to try to get a better signal.

"The signal is fine, Becca," RC said as he grabbed her hand and made her keep the phone steady. "Your phone has its Wi-Fi and produces its own signal. "Hey, Dufus!" RC raised his voice, getting Barry's attention. "Tell us what's up."

"Sorry, I've just never seen this kind of security system in a car before." Barry flipped through different software folders. "The firewall is military level. Actually, the military doesn't even have this yet."

"You're wasting time. I need you to find the folder labeled GAV17," RC instructed impatiently. "Have you found it yet?"

"Give me a second." Barry continued to flip through the folders. "Got it." He double-clicked on the folder. A password-required screen appeared. "Guys, I don't think I can bypass this password. I don't have the computing power."

Becca's hope dissipated. This was the best and only plan they had to catch up with her mother and she felt her chances of reaching her in time slipping through her fingers.

"Enter zero, one, Mike, Romeo, Golf, Lima, Override," RC said.

Becca looked at RC and her hope returned in an instant. She watched Barry type in the password. She heard a strange beep come from his side of the hologram.

"That worked!" Barry shouted.

"Find the folder that says Tracking Device and copy the serial number," RC instructed.

"Got it." Barry's hologram flickered again.

"Now input the serial number into the location software I had you install earlier and..."

"Run the number and that will pinpoint the vehicle's location," Barry interrupted. "I know what I'm doing."

Becca caught RC's disapproving look at Barry's interruption. She just smiled back at RC with a shrug. She was used to Barry's over-excitement. He always interrupted people when he was two steps ahead of them. Especially when they were trying to instruct him on something. He did that all the time with her. At first, it was annoying, but the more she worked with him the more she got used to it and realized it was a good thing. It meant he was focused and in the zone.

"Okay, I've got something. Your mom's car is located approximately fifteen miles northeast from your current location. I'm sending you the GPS coordinates now."

Becca watched as the video monitor in the car flickered and showed a new destination with a direct route how to get there.

"Great job, Barry." Becca's voice was louder than she realized due to excitement. No approval of any kind came from RC.

"Thanks, Becca. Anything else I can help you with? This was too fun."

"We need you to piggyback their coms signal so we know what's happening right now." RC kept everyone on task.

"Can we do that?" Becca asked, surprised. In all honesty, technology was not her strongest suit.

RC didn't acknowledge Becca. Instead, he continued to instruct Barry how to access the squad's communication signal. Hacking into the GPS of their car turned out to be difficult because RC wasn't sure of the call sign for Vivian's squad. RC had Barry try multiple configurations that ended with no result.

"Try Golf, November, Victor, Seven," RC said, desperately trying to get the right configuration.

Becca watched Barry's face as he waited for the computer to connect. She'd become used to him saying no connection.

It startled her when he said, "I think I've got a signal."

Becca waited for a moment. "We don't hear anything." Excitement took control of her emotions.

"I'm not hearing much on my end either," Barry said. "It's kind of garbled, but I'm definitely connected to some sort of feed."

"Well, patch us through so we can hear too," RC demanded.

"Right." Barry went back to rapidly typing on his computer and suddenly the speakers in the stolen car turned on and they heard nature sounds, no voices.

"Is this correct?" Becca asked RC.

"Shhhh!" He quieted Becca while trying to listen. He did nod, confirming to Becca that they were indeed hacked into the Griffin squad's feed. They both could hear leaves rustling. They didn't hear a voice for a good long while. Not even a breath.

"Alpha in position," a female voice said quietly.

"That's her! That's Mom." Becca jumped in her seat.

"Quiet, Becca," RC scolded.

Becca regained control of herself. She wasn't offended by his bluntness. If they were in any other type of situation that didn't involve life or death, she would speak her mind to RC about his rude tone, yet she knew this was no time for childish attitudes or inexperience. RC's demeanor proved her own suspicions correct. She really shouldn't be there, even though, through some twisted logic, the safest place for her to be was with RC.

"Bravo, Charlie, and Echo are in position," a male voice said from the feed.

"Show me video," Vivian said quietly.

"Barry, we need that video feed too," RC ordered.

"How am I supposed to send you three signals?" he asked.

"Send it to Becca's phone," RC instructed.

Becca looked at RC, confused. "Won't we lose the signal with Barry?"

"No," RC said, annoyed. "Think of it like keeping multiple apps open on an iPhone. We can do the same thing with video feeds."

Becca saw a holographic notification appear at the top right of Barry's hologram.

"Just tap it like you would a touch screen," RC told her.

Becca placed her finger in the notification box feeling nothing but air and instantly a new holographic window appeared showing a video feed from one of the Griffin squad members. Barry's projected image shrank to a smaller size allowing the new video window to be the main focus. It was a holographic Picture-in-Picture setup.

"Where's my audio, Charlie?" Vivian's voice said as thermal imagery showed a random cabin in the middle of the woods. Inside were at least seven people. All men. The outline of Edward Lake was easy to spot, as he was the only one not carrying an automatic weapon.

Becca noticed that the other men with her father were not the typical guards dressed in suits she'd encountered when she first got involved in this mess. The other six men were dressed like the fox-masked assassin who almost killed RC and Becca at Aleksi's father's condo.

"That's not good," RC said.

"Awaiting your orders, Alpha," a squad member's voice whispered.

"Hold," Becca heard her mother say. "I want to see what he's planning before we move in. Keep an eye out for the package."

Becca still wasn't used to her mother's authoritative position. She had the feeling she wasn't going to get used to it any time soon.

One of the fox assassins handed something to Edward Lake on the screen. Becca watched her father take the unidentifiable object and put it on his head while the assassins formed a circle around him.

"What are they doing?" Becca asked.

"They gave him a fox mask," RC said. "They're doing some sort of ceremony from the looks of it."

"A ceremony for what?" Barry's hologram buzzed.

Becca watched the video feed as multiple screens appeared around Edward Lake in between each assassin. On those screens appeared more fox-masked individuals. No doubt, they must be the heads of the Brotherhood.

"Thank you, Barry," RC interrupted. "Your job is done. I need you to delete the programs you downloaded and completely erase your hard drive."

"What? Why?" Barry protested. "I can continue helping."

"It's for your own safety," RC scolded.

"Becca!" Barry pleaded.

"Do it, Barry. Listen to RC."

"Fine."

The car came to a complete stop and RC turned the lights off. "We go the rest of the way on foot," RC said. He looked at Barry's flickering image. "Good job, man."

"Thanks." Barry began to plead but RC swiped his hologram window away, ending the broadcast and leaving only the video and audio from the Griffin squad projected.

"You could be a little nicer to him next time," Becca said.

"If we make it to next time," RC corrected.

"Alpha, I have eyes on the package," another male voice said.

Becca and RC returned their attention to the video. The camera zoomed in on the metal box Edward Lake had stolen from Becca. He pulled out the Royal Danish Egg and held it up for all in the room to see.

"Gentlemen, my brothers," he began, showing the egg to each monitor. "Another priceless piece of our glorious history recaptured. Today we complete our Brotherhood's noble undertaking. Today we right a very terrible wrong. Behold, Fabergé's Royal Danish Egg. Crafted for Nicholas II of Russia and gifted to his mother, Maria Feodorovna, the Dowager Empress. It is famously known to the world to contain two portraits of the Empress' parents, Christian IX of Denmark and his dear wife Louise of Hesse-Kassel."

Becca scoffed under her breath. "Everyone knows that."

"Shhhh." RC quieted Becca while not looking away from the live video as he watched Edward Lake's little victory show.

"This egg, my brothers, contains proof that exposes the truth to a secret that has eluded our Brotherhood for far too long. Today we right the wrong that happened so many years ago."

When Edward pulled out the picture, everyone in the room and on the monitors gasped. Instead of the pictures of King Christian IX of Denmark and his wife, Louise of Hesse-Kassel, there was one picture, not two.

"That looks like Grand Duchess Anastasia Nikolaevna, but older," Becca said.

21

"The Anastasia? She was killed in 1918. The girl in the photo is too old," RC said. Becca and RC were glued to the monitor, watching Edward.

"My Brothers, our rivals were clever," Edward continued. "We were deceived into believing we had eliminated the entire line of the weak Tsar Nicholas II's family in order to expand control of our Russian territory. But as we discovered in the late sixties, their lovely daughter eluded us. With only a message left behind by our enemies, her legacy lives within the egg."

Edward raised the picture again.

"Behold the proof of our mistake," Edward said. "Young Anastasia depicted at age thirty-five. A cruel taunt by our enemy. But with today's technology, their taunt becomes our gain. Now, through facial recognition and the algorithmic process of elimination, we can determine who the living descendants of Anastasia are and finish what we began over one hundred years ago. This is crucial to the Brotherhood's control over Russian territory. If this news became public and verified, we'd expose our organization to the world, and lose our control. Not only over Russia, but eventually our other territories as well.

"Our only solution to ensure the Brotherhood's control is to identify each potential descendant of Anastasia's line and remove them from the playing field."

Just then a Griffin radio squawked.

"What do we do, boss?" one of the Griffins asked.

"Hold. Just keep your eyes on Lake and the egg," Becca's mother responded.

"Stay sharp, Becca," RC said. "This could go south really quick."

Becca didn't know how she could focus. In the span of a few days, she'd found a lost Fabergé egg, learned of two secret organizations and uncovered a secret that could change history.

She didn't know how RC did it. In under a second, he'd compartmentalized a mind-blowing revelation that changed everything, and went back to what was happening at the moment. Becca let out a deep, calming sigh and glanced at the screen in the car.

Edward had the same fancy electronic equipment that Mason had in his house. Becca and RC watched a Brotherhood follower scan the picture into a hologram that had popped up in the middle of the room.

"Retrieve the egg and its contents. Move!" Vivian's voice announced over the radio.

"Roger that!" a Griffin squad member replied.

Becca and RC watched Vivian's squad quickly move closer to the cabin where Edward Lake and his Brotherhood members stood. Within seconds, all hell broke loose.

Automatic gunfire echoed so loudly, Becca heard it from inside the car as well as through the monitor. She watched members of the Brotherhood fall to the ground injured from the gunfire as her mom's squad surrounded them. She watched in horror as a fox assassin made quick work of one of the Griffins, slicing his throat. The assassin quickly grabbed the egg and ran from the cabin in Becca and RC's direction.

"Come on!" RC yelled to Becca as he hurried out the driver's side door. "We can cut him off." Becca shut off the monitor and ran after RC into the woods.

"Do not let him pass you," RC yelled while limping and running as fast as he could, considering his injury. "Get the flashlight on your phone ready!"

"What for? He'll see us," Becca exclaimed.

They slowed down behind a massive tree trunk. "Only when we want him to," he said.

"What?" She had no idea what RC was talking about.

"I need you to get in front of him and quickly aim your flashlight at his mask. Usually, the Brotherhood members have night vision goggles in their gear and I'm willing to bet this guy does."

"What if he doesn't?" Becca worried.

"Then I'll sneak up behind him anyway."

They heard running footsteps rustling in the brush. Becca worried that the assassin might see them behind the tree trunk.

"Now, Becca!" RC yelled.

The assassin looked in the direction of RC. Becca leaped out in front of him and immediately flashed the camera light from her phone right at the creepy fox mask. The assassin dropped the egg box and grasped his eyes. He removed his mask and Becca could tell that the plan had worked.

RC didn't hesitate and tackled the man. Together they struggled and grappled with each other, rolling around in the dirt.

Becca grabbed the box with the egg.

RC rolled over the assassin and wrapped his legs around the assassin's neck, gripping him tightly. He let out a groan from the pain he subjected to his injured leg, so RC used his good leg to strengthen his hold. The man struggled to get RC off him, but RC had the advantage and trapped the assassin's arms, making it impossible for him to move. RC quickly twisted his legs and the assassin went limp.

Becca watched RC struggle to his feet, lean against a tree trunk to catch his breath and run his hands over his healing injury. Then he brushed leaves and dirt off himself. He limped over to Becca. "Do you have it?"

"Yes."

Gunfire sounded from the cabin in the distance.

They raced to the car and RC started the engine.

"What are you doing?" Becca asked.

"We have to get the egg back to headquarters." RC put the car in reverse and floored it, not wasting any time.

"What about my mother and the rest of the squad?" Becca asked, frightened by the thought of leaving her mother behind. "What if they need our help?"

"They can take care of themselves." RC checked in the rear-view mirror to see if they were being followed. They weren't.

Becca turned on the video feed of her mother and the Griffin squad. "Go back," she said.

"No way! Are you nuts? Why?" RC kept his focus on the road.

"Because they've captured my mother!" Becca stared at the video projection of her mother being held by two fox assassins standing across from Edward Lake. She watched in horror as Edward touched Vivian's face gently, then hit her with the butt of his gun in the back of her head, knocking her out.

With a blazing hot rage, Becca saw red.

"Turn the car around, NOW!"

22

"There's nothing we can do, Becca!" RC yelled. "We have to get the egg away from here. Your mother understands the importance of the mission. You should too."

Becca didn't give a rat's ass about the egg or the stupid mission. The one person she had never been so wrong about in her life, her mother, was now being held captive by the one person on the planet she despised more than anything, her father. She would never forgive herself if something happened to her mother. Never. Becca opened the passenger side door of the car while it was speeding.

"What the hell are you doing?" RC shouted.

"I'm going back to save her." Becca was hell-bent, and she didn't care what it would take to accomplish her goal.

"You'll break something if you jump! You could kill yourself! How will that help your mother? Be reasonable, for God's sake. We finally have the upper hand. They won't kill her."

His words stopped her from jumping. "You don't know that for sure. You don't know him, how he is."

"He's a high-value target in the Brotherhood. I know the Brotherhood's tactics. Now get back inside before you become no use to anyone. Especially Vivian."

Becca hesitated for a good long moment. RC was right. Again.

"Damn it." She closed the passenger door and fastened her seatbelt. Becca didn't say anything for a few moments as her rage still blazed through her. She focused on her breathing to calm down.

RC broke the silence. "They will only kill your mother if they have the egg. As long as we keep it away from them your mother is safe."

"Safe?" Becca couldn't believe how nonchalantly RC took the situation. "That monster of a man gets off on beating my mother. He does it for pure joy. He will torture her within an inch of her life. He doesn't care. If anything, he will use the fact that we have the egg as motivation to abuse her. So please, don't tell me my mother is safe."

"She's stronger than you know, Becca." RC attempted to calm her down. "Give her more credit, and don't give your father as much credit."

"What is that supposed to mean?" Becca hated the fact that RC didn't seem to sympathize with her. If he did, he had a very strange way of showing it. "He's a terrible human being."

"He's simply flesh and bone, which means he can and will be destroyed. You're terrified of him. Don't be. As long as you're afraid of him he wins."

He did have a point. She still desperately wanted to return to the cabin where her mother was held, even though she'd probably be killed trying to save her. The equations going through Becca's mind on what she could do to save her mother were endless. However, every equation ended with the same outcome of probable failure. She knew she had to follow RC's lead.

"I'm sorry, Becca," RC said. "I'm more concerned about playing the cards in our favor to negotiate your mother's release. Besides, she's a Griffin. For all we know, she's already worked out her escape plan."

"You'd better be right." Becca's tone was unforgiving. Trusting the word of a stranger never sat well with her. She hated that she had to put her faith in RC's field experience.

She wanted to be able to find a solution to any problem in order to provide a better life for herself and her mother. That was one of the many reasons why she was so focused on her education. Get the best degree, then the best job. Earn a lot of money to support her and take her mother away from her father. Now, she had no idea how to help her mother. This wasn't the kind of problem she could solve on paper.

They drove through most of the night to a five-star hotel in Moscow. Becca didn't say much as all she thought about was her mother. They let the valet take their car and Becca noticed the faint brand on the valet's right wrist. It was the shape of a feather. Easily missed if you weren't looking for it.

The valet wasn't a valet at all. He was a member of the Griffins, and Becca decided he was there to get rid of the stolen car. It amazed and terrified her at the same time. Becca followed RC into the fancy lobby and up to the check-in counter. They went right into the VIP line and passed all the other customers.

Becca watched the front desk clerk perk up when he saw RC.

"Ah. Mr. Carter. Good to see you again. Your room has already been prepared." She saw that he also had a brand; this one was in the shape of a wing.

"Come on, Becca," RC said. She followed him and the front desk clerk to the elevator.

The clerk stepped inside and pressed the button for the highest floor. He held it for five seconds. After it scanned his thumbprint, he stepped out of the elevator and motioned for them to go in. "Enjoy your stay, Mr. Carter."

The doors closed silently and Becca watched the numbers rise as they went to the top floor and stopped at the penthouse.

Becca followed RC into the gigantic room. The entire floor was the suite. Kitchen, living room, multiple bedrooms, stunning view of Moscow, piano, you name it, the penthouse had it. RC didn't seem to notice. This was nothing new for him.

"Our meals should be ready," RC said. "Go eat and I'll catch up with you in a second. Kitchen is just over there." He pointed to her left and up some steps.

As Becca walked up the steps she realized when RC said kitchen, he meant restaurant with a chef and a waiter. There, sitting on a table just for her was a gourmet, American-style cheeseburger. Made to absolute perfection. Truly the best thing she had seen in all the chaos of being with RC. She sat down and took a big bite. It was delicious.

RC entered the kitchen with Winston, the butler from his house. Winston was carrying the box containing Fabergé's egg.

"Good to see you again, Miss Lake," Winston said in a very genuine and professional manner.

RC sat across from Becca. A waiter immediately brought him a succulent steak dinner. RC dug in.

"I thought you were still in New York," Becca said to Winston.

"Oh, I just arrived," he said, placing the box in the middle of the table. Winston stood between Becca and RC. "I grant you that I wish it was under better circumstances, but nonetheless it is nice to change one's scenery."

"Father sent Winston over immediately when he heard we had found the egg," RC informed Becca in between bites of his steak. "There's no one he trusts more to transfer the actual lost artifact to safety than him."

"More than you." Becca made a jab at RC who didn't acknowledge her, he just continued to eat his dinner.

"Oh indeed," Winston confirmed. "Ever since the incident with King Tut's tomb—"

"Winston!" RC interrupted. "Need to know," he scolded.

"Of course, sir," Winston said with a small smile and a quick wink to Becca.

"Wait, you found King Tut's tomb?" Becca asked RC in disbelief. "I thought that was found way before you were born."

"It was," RC confirmed. "In 1922. It was stolen again, and I was tasked with acquiring it for the museum."

"If it was stolen and found again then why is it touring the world waiting for someone to steal it another time?" Becca didn't understand the logic.

RC took a bite of his steak. "The one on tour is a replica. The real one is safely under Griffin protection."

"We're lucky it lasted after the amount of damage it suffered from transportation," Winston chimed in.

RC glared at Winston again. "Can we continue with the task at hand, please?"

Becca made a mental note to ask Winston about the rest of the story regarding RC and King Tut's tomb. "What is the plan for the egg anyway?"

"DIANA, please scan the photograph for forensics," Winston said.

Scanning.

DIANA's automated voice announced out of nowhere, startling Becca. She shouldn't have been surprised that DIANA was installed everywhere. She watched lasers scan the box. When the lasers finished, Winston opened the box with gloved hands and took out the egg. He lifted the top, pulled the photo out, and laid it on the table next to the egg. DIANA scanned the egg and Winston gently put it back into the box. DIANA then scanned the photo and projected it for all to see.

"Patch us through to Mason Carter," RC said. A hologram of Mason appeared next to the image of the egg and the photo.

"Well done in retrieving the egg with my son, Miss Lake," Mason said. "Your mother is alive and her tracking device is activated. We are currently formulating an extraction plan for her. Don't worry. We will keep you informed when there's something to report."

Those weren't exactly the words Becca hoped to hear, but it was better than nothing. "Thank you, Mr. Carter."

Scan complete, DIANA informed.

"Run facial recognition. Establish a family tree," Winston said.

Loading, DIANA announced.

RC finished his meal and wiped his mouth with his napkin. "Are you receiving this, Dad?" he asked.

"Yes. Transmission is secure," Mason responded.

"You're using facial recognition to locate every potential living descendant of Anastasia," Becca said.

"Exactly," Winston confirmed.

"There were thousands of surviving Romanovs," RC said. "Those from aunts and uncles to other distant relatives. Who knows how many are still alive. This will narrow our search to today's living members. It'll be about 90% accurate."

"I'm going to tell you something we've just discovered," Mason said while they waited for the results. "Until today most of the Griffins thought there were no surviving descendants from Anastasia. There couldn't be since she supposedly died at seventeen. What we've learned since your friend Aleksi died, was that his grandfather, Oleg Bogatir, was a loyal Griffin who was tasked to be the sole Griffin protector of Anastasia's family when the political revolution happened in 1917. Oleg was the one who got Anastasia out."

"But how?" Becca asked, fascinated. "It's common knowledge she and her family were murdered in Yekaterinburg, Russia."

"The night of the assassinations," Mason said, "Oleg smuggled Anastasia out of their home undetected. She had grabbed her grandmother's favorite decoration to remember her family by."

"The Royal Danish Egg," Becca said.

"Indeed," Mason confirmed. "Oleg vowed to go back for the rest of her family, but he was too late. Their bodies were later found in the cellar.

"Oleg decided to hide the secret of Anastasia and the egg until he could pass it on to his son at the right time. Oleg worked at the Kremlin as a carpenter in the 1930s. He foresaw the coming of the Second World War and knew the Nazis would eventually steal the egg or, worse, discover Anastasia's existence. It was Anastasia who had a self-portrait taken and swapped out the original pictures of King Christian IX and Louise of Hesse-Kassel for her own. Oleg oversaw the sealing of the well and hid the egg inside, forever burying the secret of Anastasia's survival. Oleg carried this secret his whole life. He only told his son, Ivan, Aleksi's father, on his deathbed. Ivan did the same, giving Aleksi a deathbed confession."

"That's why Aleksi was killed," Becca said quietly.

"Yes, we think so," Mason said. "If Anastasia survived, which by the looks of things she might have, there'd be one or two generations of offspring."

Becca watched as potential candidates appeared next to photos of Anastasia. Three photos appeared. The program continued to search for more descendants. It amazed Becca that these people were unknowingly related to the most famous member of the Romanov family.

A few more photos of women appeared. Some you could tell were daughters of others. DIANA's algorithm showed a percentage of probability for each person. Most were in the 20% to 30% ratio. Two more portraits appeared and the search stopped.

Search complete, DIANA said.

RC immediately stood. His eyes wide with shock and disbelief. Winston stared at the last two photos. Both were women. Both with dark hair and dark eyes.

"My God," the projection of Mason said with complete surprise.

Becca also shared everyone's shock as she stood and stared at the final two photos. There, projected in front of everyone in the room, were photos of Vivian Lake and Rebecca Hunter Lake, each with a 90% match under their faces.

23

Silence spread through the room as Becca stared dumbfounded at the projected photos of her and her mother next to Anastasia.

"Impossible," was the only word she could manage to break the silence.

RC, Mason, and Winston immediately discussed a new plan of action but it sounded jumbled to Becca. She was way too distracted by the possibility of her relationship to Anastasia. She continued to stare at the probability number projected under her photo and the 90% that floated in front of her.

Mason's voice broke Becca's concentration. "Staff. I need you to clear the room." Without question or protest, the chef and waiters left the kitchen, leaving the vast area to Winston, RC, and Becca.

"This can't get out. At all," Mason stated. "If this newfound information reached the Brotherhood, any hope of getting Vivian out of there safely is lost."

"What do we do about Becca?" RC asked.

"We have to keep her safe," Mason said. "If the Brotherhood sent out an elimination notice for the Romanovs in 1918 and their followers didn't complete the task, they will likely kill each remaining descendant of Anastasia to cover their failure. We need to find any DNA evidence from anything Anastasia may have touched while she was alive or any artifact that survived the massacre. No matter what, once the picture surfaces, Becca and Vivian's resemblance to Anastasia, no matter how slight it is, will cause speculation among Internet conspiracy theorists that will prove detrimental to our plans. All the world needs to see is the 90% number to go crazy."

The importance of containing the secret didn't go unnoticed. Becca felt like she was in a police interrogation room wondering if she'd ever taste freedom again.

Winston walked up to Becca. His demeanor was surprisingly comforting.

"Please swab your cheek, Miss Lake," Winston said as if nothing groundbreaking had happened in the room, "in case any artifact turns up that we may use to compare to your DNA sample." It was just another day in the office for him.

"Oh, of course." Becca used the swab-tipped stick and handed it to Winston who placed it into a sealed container, labeled it, and took it to be analyzed.

RC and Mason continued to discuss tactics about how to rescue Vivian.

"What are the chances that DIANA is wrong?" she interrupted. Doubt had taken over her thought process. Might have been denial.

"Not likely," Mason replied, then returned to strategizing with RC.

No comfort there, Becca thought.

"I'll make some tea to calm the nerves." Winston went into the kitchen.

"I think it's safe to say you can kiss any life plans you might've had goodbye, Becca," RC said, nonchalantly. "Keeping you alive just went from a personal kindness to priority number one. That is until we get your father off your back."

Becca felt light-headed. She sank into the chair at the table across from RC with her head in her hands.

"Same for your mother," Mason chimed in. "We don't have time to waste. This information has to be kept from the Brotherhood at all costs. RC, you will rendezvous with a new squad immediately. By the time you arrive with them, your rescue strategy will be intact. Rebecca, I want you on the next flight back to New York with Winston as your escort."

"No way. I'm going with RC to get my mom back." She caught the look on RC's face that admired her courage.

"It's non-negotiable," Mason said. "You're in too much danger and I won't allow you to put yourself in harm's way."

Becca looked at RC for any help in swaying Mason's decision but all he did was shrug, assuring her that there was nothing he could do. It was clearly out of his hands.

Winston returned with the tea in a travel mug and Becca didn't feel like taking a sip. Any decision she made for herself in the immediate future would have to be filtered and approved by others. She already despised the thought.

"Don't worry, Becca," RC said as he stood to his feet. "I'll get her back."

"That almost sounded like a promise." Becca stared at him and felt as if there was an unspoken trust between them. No matter their differences and moral choices, she knew RC would do his best to get her mother back safely. Becca couldn't help but wish there was a way she could go with him.

Her cell phone rang and the caller ID read Mom.

Becca immediately answered it on speaker. "Mom! Are you okay?" She was desperate to hear her mother's voice. There was a moment's pause and then she heard it...

"Hello, Rebecca," the deep baritone and disgusting sound of Edward Lake's voice responded.

"Where is she, you bastard?" Becca felt like she could rip her cell phone in half.

"Don't waste your breath with meaningless threats, Rebecca. Your inexperience makes any point of view you might have invalid and not worth my attention. With one word I can have you and your mother eliminated and neither of you will ever see it coming. I'm only speaking to you for your pathetic Griffin allies to listen in on my requests."

Becca looked at RC and saw he was motioning for her to breathe and not lose her temper. Her father's insults were intolerable, but RC was right. She needed to control her emotions to the best of her ability, which was no easy task. "What do you want?"

"I propose a trade. Today. Your mother for the photo that was in the egg along with all the information the Griffins have deduced by now about any living descendants."

Becca looked to RC, who was shaking his head negatively.

"I need an answer, girl," her father said. "Now."

Stalling, Becca said, "I need a moment. I'm not the one to negotiate with." After a long sigh, Becca said, "Okay."

Her phone received a text. She opened it and saw it was an address.

"I've sent you the coordinates for the trade. You have two hours to be there. If you fail to give me what I want...well, you know what happens."

"I'll be there," she said into the phone.

"Excellent. You can bring a few of your Griffin friends with you. I know it's pointless to request you come alone because no one ever does. Even in the regular governments." He hung up.

"Are you insane?" RC growled to Becca as soon as the line went dead. He looked ready to strangle someone. "We can't protect you now. You should never have agreed to his terms."

"We can have a double for Rebecca ready in thirty minutes," Mason said. "But that won't get her to the location on time."

"We can't let her go through with this," RC stated flatly.

"We don't have a choice," Mason said. "Rebecca, my organization can no longer guarantee your safety. I want to make sure that you are fully aware of the danger you're in."

"She has no idea what she's doing." RC didn't try to hide his true feelings about the negotiations. "This is a terrible idea."

"You're right," Becca said as she paced around the room, then looked at RC. She felt a strange bit of blind confidence overcome her. "I have no idea what I'm doing and honestly I don't care. That bastard has my mother and I will do anything to get her back. Anything. You have technology and people all over the world with secrets and skills I would never think were possible. I know you will use them to the best of your ability. However, I will not sit back and hide while waiting for someone to tell me whether my mother makes it out dead or alive. Regardless of my lack of experience."

"He will most likely kill you and your mother the moment you arrive at the trade point," Mason said. "You're not dealing with anyone close to resembling a normal human being. Brotherhood members do not value life. They value status and material items only. This is their common trait. They will cross each other if it means winning. There's no honor among thieves. None. Therefore, the fact that you have agreed to a meeting in a place where we have no time to recon for kill zones puts us at an extreme disadvantage. DIANA, tell Miss Lake what the probability of her getting out of this situation alive is."

Mission success probability 35%, DIANA informed.

"You've basically signed your own death warrant," RC said.

Becca didn't say anything for a moment. "I need a copy of the living descendants for the delivery."

"Are you just blatantly not listening now?" RC was furious. "Becca, it's suicide."

"Maybe. But it's also a way for you to bring down the Brotherhood."

She watched as that statement diffused some of the tension in the room.

"How do you mean?" Mason asked.

"RC showed me a way to hack into the car video feed to piggyback the Griffin signal of my mom's squad."

"So?" RC shrugged in anger.

"You can put a tracking program in the data I hand over to piggyback the network of the Brotherhood. While they're searching for the location of all the living descendants, the Griffins will be pinpointing all locations of the Brotherhood and its members."

Becca watched the image of Mason sit back in his office chair, deeply thinking about her approach. "It's dangerous but possible."

"There's still no guarantee of you getting out alive," RC said. "Saying you're ready to die is one thing compared to actually being ready to die."

"If I'm going to be killed by my own father, then I'm going to make sure I destroy everything he values."

"I admire your courage, Rebecca," Mason said. "I really do. I promise I'll surround you with the best team we have."

"Thank you," she replied, genuinely terrified of what was about to come. She looked at RC, whose entire demeanor reeked of disapproval. "What do you say? Protect me one last time?"

"You don't have to ask," he said. "It's my job."

She was hoping for a random bit of encouragement from RC and this was the first time he didn't seem confident about the upcoming mission. In the few weeks she'd known him, he'd always had a way of seeing the small chance of success. Not this time. This time she might have made the worst decision of her life. She wasn't ready to die and she didn't understand how anyone could be.

24

The coordinates that Edward Lake had sent led Becca to an executive terminal at Sheremetyevo International Airport. She sat in the backseat of the limousine with RC sitting to her right as they rode to their destination. It felt like the longest drive she'd ever been on.

Becca was terrified, and she didn't care who knew it. However, she was more terrified that she'd fail to get her mother back. The entire related-to-Anastasia thing hadn't had a chance to sink in.

RC monitored the airport entrances and exits using some special software through DIANA. It was a little over Becca's head, but she knew he was checking for possible Brotherhood of the Fox key positioning.

"They could have snipers on the east roof." He pointed to it. "The gate guards could very well be foxes in disguise. I don't like this at all. There are too many places that become a kill box. For all we know, they've already taken over the entire airport."

"Can they do that?" Becca asked.

"They've done it with Heathrow in the past. I only heard about it." He picked up his cell phone and began making demands for more units to scope out certain areas of the airport.

As the information came in, the map that DIANA used to help RC strategize became clearer, almost like a puzzle getting all its pieces together.

For a moment Becca forgot she held the Royal Danish Egg in her lap. She opened it and looked at the photo of Anastasia. There really was a spooky resemblance between them. She saw a few of her mother's features as well as her own, meaning Anastasia could be her great-grandmother.

Looking deeper into the gravity of what it meant made her feel incredibly uncomfortable. Instead, she chose to come up with a more logical explanation to calm her nerves. There had to be some sort of glitch in DIANA's programming. The photo of Anastasia was photoshopped and aged, or something. The second seemed more likely than the first.

The more she denied the possibility of her relation to Anastasia, the less logical her deductions became. Instead, she found more questions in her head than answers, which did nothing for her nerves.

"Don't do that," RC said to Becca.

She looked at him confused. "What?"

"Try to find a reason to explain this," he said.

She almost blushed. "How could you tell that's what I was doing?"

He responded to a text while he answered. "Some people in the world wear their hearts on their sleeves, you wear your thoughts on your face, which makes you the furthest thing from a sphinx."

A sphinx. Someone who keeps their thoughts to themselves, Becca remembered. He was right. Her entire life she hadn't been able to hide her thoughts and emotions. She'd had countless arguments with her mother over that very same thing. "I don't know how to handle all of this. It's not normal," she said.

"First thing you have to learn about this life is that nothing is normal. The most extraordinary finds, battles, thefts, and recoveries never happen with any form of normalcy." He finished sending his text. "Betrayal and death are common."

"You're not normal," she said, attempting to make a joke.

"There's nothing more boring than normal," he said. "It's harsh, but it's true."

"I agree with you there," Becca said.

"Don't," he said. "It's just weird."

"Why is it weird?"

He put his phone down and looked her right in the eyes. "If you agree with me that means you're not normal. I'm used to risking my life for the adventure and to save the lives of normal people who have no concept of what I truly do. But when you agree with me it means you understand what I do. It makes me uncomfortable."

"You're not making any sense."

He hesitated for a second. RC looked embarrassed for what he was about to say. "I was getting used to protecting you as a normal person."

"That almost sounded like a compliment," Becca said.

"Don't get ahead of yourself. I'm just saying my job has more demands than usual right now. The more you get used to everything not being what your definition of normal is, the better your chances of survival will be."

Becca took his words to heart. "I think you're full of it," she said. "I think you're just as nervous about the trade as I am."

"Nervous?" he replied. "I wouldn't say nervous."

"Terrified," she corrected.

RC didn't respond.

"We're here," the driver said as he looked into the rearview mirror.

"Game time, everybody," RC said. His face stilled and his eyes narrowed. Whenever she saw that look Becca thought of it as his focused mode. He was preparing for war and nothing would get in the way. "Everyone have their protective vests on? This could get ugly." Becca patted her chest and the driver gave a thumbs-up.

The car pulled up to the executive terminal gate and a guard motioned them through.

"Is he one of yours?" Becca asked RC.

"No. I've never seen him before," he replied. "He could just actually work here." RC kept his attention on the holographic map in the car. "Remember, Becca. Not everyone is a member of the Brotherhood or the Griffins. There are just regular people here too."

After learning about the two secret organizations, Becca felt as if everybody belonged to one or the other. No one looked innocent anymore.

Straight ahead of them was a helicopter pad and two black cars. Standing in front of the vehicles were three men, all in heavy trench coats. In the middle stood Edward Lake, proud and menacing. Becca felt disgust as she looked at him. She grasped the box containing the egg. "Where's Mom?" Becca worried.

"I don't know," RC replied. "Anyone have eyes on Vivian?" RC listened to his earbuds but eventually shook his head at Becca, confirming there was no sign of her.

"Then I'm not leaving the car until I see her," Becca said.

"Good," RC said. "Let's just hope they don't blow us up since we are sitting ducks parked here."

"Not helping the nerves," Becca said.

"Sir." The driver pointed to Edward Lake.

Becca and RC watched Edward Lake nod to one of his men. The side door of the helicopter slid open and Vivian Lake, bruised and beaten, with a cloth tied around her mouth, began to step out.

"Mom!" Becca watched her mother be shoved out of the helicopter by Edward's henchman. She fell to the ground. As she struggled to stand, the Brotherhood followers next to her made her lean forward on her knees facing Edward, like a supplicant waiting for a response from God. Becca gritted her teeth.

Edward held out a hand toward Vivian showing Becca and RC that she was alive, for the time being, and then motioned for them to come to him.

"I'll go first," RC told Becca. He slowly opened the door and exited the limo. He left the door open for Becca but waved a hand for her to stay inside the car.

She watched as RC looked around, checking to see if the area was clear. Well, as clear as it could be. He then motioned for the driver to exit, which he did, and after a few moments of double-checking, he said, "All right, Becca. Now or never."

Becca took in a deep breath before getting out of the limo. She held on to the box tightly as RC escorted her toward Edward. RC walked in front of her, acting as a shield for snipers, and the driver walked behind Becca for the same reason.

"If I wanted to shoot you, I would have done it already," Edward said. "My photo?" he pointed to the box.

"You okay, Mom?" Becca asked.

Vivian nodded but had a very concerned look in her eyes.

"She's alive. You have my photo. Give it to me now."

"Give me my mother first." Becca looked right into Edward's eyes, not afraid of him. Her knees were shaking. She might not be afraid of her father, but she was afraid of being shot.

"Very well." Edward nodded to one of his henchmen. The man roughly grabbed Vivian and brought her to her feet. She was weak from the beating she had sustained.

"No!" Becca demanded. "Let her walk to me by herself." She saw the rage in Edward's eyes. He didn't like taking demands from anyone, especially not from her, his eighteen-year-old daughter.

Edward nodded, allowing Becca's request to be fulfilled. The man let go of Vivian and she slowly walked toward Becca, pain evident in every step she took.

"The photo, girl. Hand it over," Edward demanded.

Becca walked toward Edward and RC stopped her.

"Wait," he said as he grabbed her arm. "Let someone else hand it over."

Becca knew better than to argue with RC. She let him take the box to Edward Lake instead. She watched as RC and Vivian exchanged a look as they passed each other. It wasn't a confident one.

"That's far enough," Edward said, holding his hand out for RC to stop moving. "Place the box on the ground and walk away."

RC did as he was told.

Becca hugged her mother and removed the cloth from around her mouth.

"You shouldn't be here," Vivian said.

"I know. Thank God you're alive." They returned their attention to Edward and his men as they all moved up to the box.

RC returned and spoke quietly. "Get ready to make a run for the car if necessary."

Edward opened the box and saw the egg. He didn't care much about the egg and quickly opened the top, revealing the photo of Anastasia. He smiled, "And where's the data from your organization?"

Becca pulled out a flash drive from her pocket.

"No, Becca. Don't give it to him," Vivian pleaded.

"Don't listen to her," Edward's voice was stern.

Becca looked at RC for any sense of a backup plan. He shook his head negatively. He had none. Becca tossed the flash drive high into the air toward Edward Lake. He caught it and immediately handed it over to one of his henchmen, who took it into the helicopter.

"It's not encrypted," the man said after he plugged it into a laptop.

"Excellent," Edward responded.

"You have what you want," Becca said. "We're done here."

"Almost, daughter. Almost. Just need to verify that you haven't hidden any search programs in the drive. Only then will I allow you to leave."

"So far so good," Edward's man updated.

RC's phone rang. He ignored it. Then Becca's rang.

"Really, in the middle of a trade?" RC scoffed as he checked his phone. Becca noticed it wasn't just them. Edward and his henchmen's phones all went off, ringing up a storm as well.

"What the hell is going on?" Edward asked as he checked his phone.

Becca saw her father's expression change from confusion to shock. It was almost the exact same look she had seen on RC and Mason's faces when they found out Becca was most likely related to Anastasia.

"Becca…" RC said, terrified.

"What?" Becca yelled. She saw RC show her his phone with a breaking news video. The news had both Becca and Vivian's photos saying Anastasia's Bloodline Lives?

"Oh, shit!" RC said.

Becca quickly looked at Edward Lake and knew he and his men were seeing the exact same video. His expression changed from anger to pure rage.

Edward and his men all drew their weapons.

"Kill them!"

25

A flurry of gunfire erupted in an instant. The driver dove in front of Becca and her mother. His body jerked from the bullet hits before he fell to the ground. The driver struggled to his feet, gripped his chest, and coughed. His protective vest had saved his life. He gave RC the thumbs up. RC returned fire at Edward and the members of the Brotherhood, forcing them to take cover.

"GO!" RC yelled.

Vivian grabbed Becca and they ran for the limo and hid behind it. RC was right behind them with the injured driver.

"Give me a gun," Vivian said.

"In the armrest!" RC responded while firing at the Brotherhood.

Vivian provided cover while RC helped the driver into the car before turning back to fire.

RC's aim was dead on. He took out both of Edward's men by shooting them in the head. The gunfire was loud and terrifying. Becca covered her ears and kept her legs tucked in as close to her as possible.

"Becca, get inside and drive!" her mother shouted at her after firing a few more rounds to keep the Brotherhood at bay.

Becca hurried inside the limo and flinched as bullets hit the side of the car. Luckily, the car was bulletproof, but she did not know how long that would hold. She climbed from the back through the divider and saw the keys were still in the ignition. She made her way into the driver's seat and saw more Brotherhood members running toward them from the airport. Becca started the limo.

"Get in!" she yelled.

Vivian hurried into the back of the car and slightly lowered a rear window to fire back at the Brotherhood. RC stood inside the open door, steadied his gun on the roof of the limo, and fired across the top of the car.

"GO, GO, GO!" RC yelled while firing his weapon.

Becca floored the gas pedal and instead of leaving the airport, she drove directly toward the oncoming enemy.

"Where are you going? Get us out of here." RC struggled to hold on to the limo and fire his weapon.

Vivian shot two more members and opened the armrest. She took out two more magazines of bullets for her and RC. "I like where your head's at, Becca, but we only have one opportunity to stop them, then we have to get out of here. Give them hell!"

"You got it," Becca replied. She ran into as many Brotherhood members as she could using the car. One rolled onto the hood and tried firing his weapon at Becca through the windshield. Becca jumped at the gunfire and saw the bullets stick in the window. She swerved the car back and forth, forcing the fox member to lose his balance and fall off the hood.

"Take that!" she yelled. She headed straight for the tail propeller of Edward's helicopter. She slammed the brakes of the car and swerved, trying to avoid being shredded by the tail rotor.

The helicopter lifted into the air, barely missing the limo. A car skidded underneath the chopper. Becca saw her father in the cockpit. She couldn't hear him, but she could read his shouting lips. "Don't let them get away!"

"Whoa!" RC dove inside the limo. The open door was ripped off the car as it clipped one of the Brotherhood cars.

"Sorry!" Becca yelled from the driver's seat as she floored the gas pedal again.

"Just get us out of here," RC yelled.

Becca looked in the rear-view mirror and saw the cars chasing after them. "This is starting to become familiar," she said under her breath.

"Running out of ammo," Vivian said. "Becca, find us cover if you can. We need to stay away from the helicopter at all costs!"

"What about their cars?" Becca asked.

"Keep us as close to the cars as possible. Hopefully, that will force Edward to hold his fire from the helicopter."

"Got it." Becca slammed the brakes, allowing the cars to get closer, and then floored it again.

"Give us a heads-up the next time you do that, please." RC reloaded his weapon.

"My bad," Becca said.

"Becca! On your right," Vivian shouted.

Becca looked just in time to see a Brotherhood car slam against theirs. A fox member jumped from their car into the limo and battled with RC. They struggled for the gun. RC accidentally fired two shots, almost hitting both Vivian and Becca. Vivian hit the fox member on the back of his head, stunning him, then grabbed his weapon and returned to shooting the other car chasing them.

Becca saw an airplane hangar with an open door straight ahead. She turned the wheel to the right forcing their car to lock up against the other. As the hangar got closer the other car didn't give up, which was exactly what she counted on.

"Come on," Becca said to herself, focused. She quickly steered the wheel to the left and then back to the right causing the limo to slam back into the Brotherhood's car. The other driver struggled to maintain control of his vehicle. Becca steered the limo away from the Brotherhood car just in time to enter the hangar and have their enemy crash into the side of the hangar door.

"Nice one, Becca," RC yelled from the back as he threw the

stunned fox member out of the moving limo. "Remind me to never let you drive me anywhere if we make it through this."

"Deal," Becca said.

"We still have another car on our tail," Vivian said. She fired at the tires but it didn't stop them. "Their tires are reinforced. We need a plan."

A barrage of machine-gun fire pierced through the roof of the hangar, destroying some parked planes. Becca swerved the limo to avoid hitting a plane wing that smashed into the pursuing car. That Brotherhood car crashed into another parked plane.

"What was that?" Becca asked.

"The helicopter must have armor-piercing rounds," Vivian said.

"A new kind of armor-piercing rounds," RC said.

"Please tell me we have something to deal with the helicopter or we're not going to last long in here," Becca said. "I can't circle the car all day."

"I'm on my last mag and it won't do much damage," Vivian said.

"We have the trunk gun but it's only two shots," RC said. "I'm open to suggestions."

"Does Ed have a reloadable gun?" Becca asked.

"A what?" RC responded.

"Is he able to reload the helicopter gun?" Becca reiterated.

"No," Vivian answered. "But he has a lot of ammunition and will destroy this hangar with another pass."

"Is it possible for us to outrun him and just have him waste his bullets?" Becca asked.

"There's no cover on the highway and he's too clever to waste ammunition," Vivian responded.

RC pulled the backseat of the limo down and pulled a box out of the trunk. Inside was an RPG and two rockets.

"You destroy the helicopter, you destroy the egg and all its secrets," Vivian said.

"Small price to pay, if that means we live. Plus, that's not our problem." RC loaded one rocket into the RPG. "I have to hit the damn thing first."

"Come in, RC!" Mason said over the car speakers.

"We're here. Just barely," RC said.

"Reinforcements are on their way. Draw the helicopter to us. I've sent the coordinates to the GPS," Mason said.

Becca watched the car's GPS kick into gear. The Griffin reinforcements were ten minutes away on the highway.

"I don't know if we can make it," Becca said.

"You have to. We can cover you from there. Just hold him off," Mason said.

"Those are our orders, Becca. You can do it," Vivian said.

Becca had no idea how to get them there safely, but she had to try. "I love you, Mom," she said.

"I love you too, sweetie. I'm extremely proud of you." Vivian loaded the last magazine into her weapon and faced RC.

"Save all the ammo you can," he said.

"Don't fire unless you have a clear shot," Vivian told RC.

He put the RPG on his shoulder. "We're gonna die," he said. "Floor it, Becca."

Becca aimed the limo for the hangar door. RC set up at the rear opening where the door had been ripped off, and Vivian opened the moon roof.

The limo zoomed out of the hangar, passing the destroyed planes. Becca saw the helicopter hovering to her right and immediately drove under it.

"Stay as close to the building as possible!" Vivian shouted.

"Keep swerving too!" RC added.

The helicopter returned fire, but Becca had placed the limo well, making it difficult for the barrage to be aimed directly at them. It was too close for comfort but it did make Edward's job a lot harder to fly and shoot. They swerved through and around hangars on the airport property. Every time the helicopter fired at them it destroyed the hangars, planes, and walls around them.

"Keep it up, Becca. Make him waste his ammo if you can. Taunt him," Vivian encouraged. She aimed her gun at the cockpit and fired two rounds.

Becca saw the flashes of the bullets as they hit the cockpit shield in her side-view mirror, but Edward flew effortlessly.

"I still have no shot," RC said, holding the RPG.

"I'm running out of buildings for him to destroy," Becca yelled as she drove them through the last hangar before heading to the main road.

"Fire another shot at him, Vivian," RC shouted.

She did.

Becca saw the spark of the bullet hit the cockpit shield. RC must have seen it too. He fired a rocket at the helicopter. The rocket flew toward the helicopter at a rapid pace and passed the tail blades, just missing its target by a few inches. Edward continued his pursuit of the limo.

"Shit," RC said.

Edward fired another barrage of bullets at the limo.

Becca saw the bullet spray in the rearview mirror as it shredded the asphalt, grass, and trees, causing a massive wave of debris to rapidly move closer to swallowing the limousine. She squeezed the steering wheel as tightly as she could, ready for the worst, and then it stopped.

The destructive wave behind her had dissipated.

"We're alive!" RC shouted.

"You did it, Becca!" Vivian yelled, overjoyed.

"He's out of bullets?" Becca wasn't sure what had just happened. She double-checked the rear-view mirror to make sure she was right. She could hear the helicopter still chasing them in the air. "He's out of bullets!" She screamed. "I can't believe that worked."

"We're not out of this yet," RC said, concerned.

"What's going on?" Becca shouted. "I can't see."

"Oh my God," Vivian muttered.

"Edward has men in the helicopter with him," RC said as he loaded the last rocket.

"And they have machine guns?" Becca fished for more information.

"Nope," he said calmly. "They have rocket launchers."

26

Thunderous booms startled Becca as she continued to zigzag the limousine away from the rocket launcher fire. The M11 Motorway from Moscow to St. Petersburg was getting obliterated inch by inch by Edward's helicopter.

"Where the hell are our guys?" RC shouted as he tried to get a clear shot of the helicopter. "Damn it."

The windshield shattered from debris and Becca was forced to drive while squinting from the wind that blew in. "I can't keep this up much longer!" Becca yelled from the driver's seat, avoiding another rocket launcher blast.

Vivian fired one shot from the moon roof of the car and hit a fox member. He fell from the helicopter and hit the ground. Vivian ducked back into the car. "I only have two shots left!"

"Drive straight for a second, please!" RC shouted.

"Are you nuts? We'll get blown up," she yelled back at him.

"We're about to be anyway!" RC responded. "Do it."

Becca stopped swerving the car and drove straight, praying this would work.

RC aimed the rocket launcher at the helicopter, getting it perfectly in his sights. "Vivian, the guy on the left."

Vivian fired one more shot and took out the fox member on the left side of the helicopter. "Shoot now!"

RC fired the rocket at the helicopter. "Come on. Come on!" he said. The rocket soared through the air toward its target. The helicopter banked out of the way with ease as the rocket zoomed past its target.

"Did you get him?" Becca looked in the rear-view mirror and all she saw was RC and Vivian looking at each other hopelessly.

"BRACE YOURSELF, BECCA!" Vivian shouted as she and RC dove for the seats of the limousine, grabbing seat belts.

Becca fastened hers as quickly as she could, then BOOM! The world exploded in front of her. The limo lurched and swerved then shuddered to a stop amid screeching metal and a whining engine. The airbag activated. Becca's head hit it, which caused bruises, but the airbag saved her life.

Becca's eyes focused through a blurry haze and she realized she was still alive.

"Mom...RC?" She coughed from all the dust and debris in the air. Her head pounded, she already had whiplash, and blood ran down the side of her face. She heard water from the radiator steaming. The limousine had crashed into a giant pothole created by Edward's recent rocket fire. The hood was completely demolished and the rear end of the limousine was raised in the air. She felt something out of place. Had to be a rib, maybe two.

"Becca. Becca!" Vivian shouted out of fright from the back of the car. "Can you move?"

"Yeah. I think something is broken," she said.

"It will be the first of many," RC said from the back. "We need to get out of here now."

Becca unbuckled her seatbelt, still dazed from the blast. She opened the driver's side door and tried to get out but felt something pressed on her leg.

"I'm stuck." She heard RC and Vivian scrambling in the back to get closer to her.

"I'm coming, sweetheart," Vivian said. "Just move what you can. The more you're able to do, the quicker we can help get you out."

"My...my leg is stuck." Becca struggled to get free and yelled in pain.

"We have to get out through the moon roof. Hang on, Becca." RC and Vivian climbed out of the limo.

"I'm not going anywhere." Becca sighed, trying to breathe without flinching from the pain. Vivian hurried to her side and began to free Becca's leg from the crushed dashboard and steering wheel.

"He's coming back around," RC warned.

"Help!" Vivian demanded. "Grab her arm."

RC did as he was told, keeping his eyes on the helicopter as it circled toward them. "Come on, Becca. Help us out here. Push yourself toward us with your free arm," he said.

Becca shouted in pain as she pushed her body away from the dashboard toward RC. Vivian freed Becca's foot.

"There. Move!" Vivian cleared out of Becca's way. RC picked Becca up and carried her out of the driver's seat. Becca found his strength truly impressive. He carried her out of the pothole to the main street.

"Can you walk?" he asked.

"Yes, I think so," she replied.

RC gently placed her down and all three of them looked up at the oncoming helicopter. They could see the remaining fox members on each side of the helicopter readying their rockets to fire at them.

"Well, that was fun," RC said breaking the tension.

Becca laughed with pain. His timing was terrible but things were so dire she didn't care anymore. How could she? It was amazing to her that they'd lasted even as long as they had.

"You said you have one shot left?" Becca asked her mom.

"It won't do any good against the helicopter," she said defeated.

"Aim for one of the guys' feet," Becca said.

"Becca, it won't change anything," RC reaffirmed.

"What else do we have to lose?" Becca smiled, knowing that it was completely hopeless for them.

Vivian pulled out her handgun. "She does have a point." Vivian aimed for a final time at the helicopter, this time focusing on one of the Brotherhood of the Fox men on the side. She waited for them to get closer.

Becca grabbed RC's hand and held it tightly in hers. She felt a tingling sensation go through her arm at his touch. Maybe in another life they could've been a good couple. She accepted the fact that she'd never find out.

"Thank you for doing your best to keep me alive," she said.

"It's not every day I get to save a beautiful woman." He smiled hopelessly at her.

"Take this, you bastard." Vivian fired the last bullet.

The fox member flinched as the bullet hit his foot. He jolted in pain, losing his focus, and accidentally fired the rocket launcher at the tail of the helicopter.

"TAKE COVER!" RC yelled as the helicopter spun violently out of control toward them. They all jumped into the massive pothole, ducking as the helicopter crashed onto the asphalt. The propeller scraped against the ground and cut the limousine in half as it tumbled past them, eventually stopping on the side of the motorway.

Becca, Vivian, and RC peeked out of the pothole and, to their surprise, saw that the helicopter had not exploded. But it was still in danger of doing so after the crash, with leaking fuel and some fires that were on the ground.

"We have a chance to get the egg back," Vivian said. She didn't hesitate and made a run for the helicopter.

"Mom, wait!" Becca winced in pain again as she tried to stop her mother.

RC helped Becca out of the pothole once more.

Becca looked for her mother and saw the downed helicopter.

She could see her father in the cockpit. He wasn't moving. She stared as she watched Vivian search through the wreckage for the egg box. Becca didn't have high hopes that the egg survived, but she was more concerned if Edward had. Her hopes were dashed when she saw him cough in the cockpit. Like a madman, he quickly unbuckled himself from his seat and saw Vivian not far from him.

"Mom, look out!" Becca shouted. Edward went for his handgun, but Vivian was quicker. Grabbing his wrist she twisted it, disarming him, then knocked the gun out of the helicopter.

Becca froze out of fear for her mother, as Edward didn't go easy on Vivian at all. He kicked Vivian away from the cockpit and hurried after her with violent intent. It was one of the most horrific sights Becca had ever seen. Complete and utter rage from both of them. Every strike was meant to end the opponent as swiftly as possible.

Amazingly, Vivian was able to hold her own against Edward. Becca had never seen, let alone imagined, her mother being able to fight with such strength and agility.

"Come on. She needs help." RC faced Becca and then shoved her out of the way of one of the fox members who charged at them from behind. Becca fell to the ground hard and had the air knocked out of her.

"Becca! Get the egg!" RC yelled as he fought the fox member. Becca struggled to her feet and hurried over to the helicopter while holding her painful side. She searched for the egg box. She heard the grunts and groans from the bout happening between Edward and Vivian. It made it difficult for her to search for the egg.

"It isn't here!" She looked back at the fight between Edward and Vivian and saw Edward backhand her mother, causing her to fall to the ground in pain, dazed.

Becca hurried behind him and jumped on his back, clawing at him. Pain ripped through her, but anger and desperation dulled it. He easily knocked her off him.

"Who knew? You two," Edward gloated. "The most unimportant

people on the planet in a split second..." he snapped his fingers, "become the most famous people in the world." He kicked Becca in the stomach and she fell to her knees gasping for air. Through a red haze, she saw RC fighting the fox member not too far from her as she listened to Edward talk about how ironic his life was. To be honest, she had tuned out his voice because all it did was make her angrier every time he spoke. Her eyes landed on the handgun just an arm's length away from her. The one Vivian knocked out of Edward's hand moments ago.

"Well, at least I get to kill two birds with one stone. Not only are you both a nuisance to the Brotherhood..." Edward grabbed Vivian by her hair and pulled her back painfully, making her yell in pain. "But you will never —"

BANG!

Edward fell backward, dead before he hit the ground. Becca saw Vivian open her eyes and look directly at her, realizing what had just happened.

It happened so fast. Becca had grabbed the handgun, aimed, and fired it at Edward from her knees. She had a hard time letting go of the weapon. Vivian came over to comfort her and tried to pull the gun from her hand. Becca held it tight.

"It's okay, Sweetheart. You can let go," she said gently.

Becca hesitated for a moment, staring only at Edward's lifeless body. She caught reassuring eyes with her mother and let Vivian take the gun from her. Vivian hugged Becca but she didn't feel it. She continued to stare at Edward on the ground.

"Ugh. A little help, please!" RC yelled while fighting the last fox member in the area.

Vivian quickly aimed and shot the fox in the leg and RC was able to finish him off.

"Thanks," he said as he made his way over to Becca and Vivian. It took him only a second to piece together what had happened.

"Becca..." RC began, but then multiple cars arrived at the scene, interrupting him. The Griffin squad Mason sent had finally arrived.

Armed men and women exited the vehicles and had their weapons at the ready for any more Brotherhood of the Fox surprises. One woman, clearly the one in charge of the unit, came over to them.

"Mr. Carter, Ms. Lake, are you all right?" she asked.

"That was the longest ten minutes of my life," RC replied, annoyed.

"Becca needs a medic," Vivian informed the squad leader while still holding onto her daughter.

The woman called it in and then addressed Becca, RC, and Vivian. "We need to get moving."

"No," RC corrected. "We need to find the egg."

"It's under the body," Becca said slowly and quietly, still in shock. "The dead member. His body is on top of the egg box," Becca choked up on her words. "I shot Ed."

RC removed the dead fox's body from covering the box. He opened it, surprised. "Would you look at that? It survived."

Becca didn't look at the egg. She could not remove her gaze from her father's dead body, let alone believe what had just happened, what she had done, and what that meant. It numbed her to the bone.

She felt a lack of energy mixed with a sense of relief and that's what terrified her most. Not the fact that she had just killed her father, but the fact that from now on and for the rest of their lives, she and Vivian would never have to be bothered by the disgusting Edward Lake ever again.

The relief frightened Becca the most. She had just learned that no matter what, she would do whatever needed to be done to save her family and her friends, even if that meant taking a life. She now knew she had a caged ruthlessness inside her that had finally been set free.

27

Becca didn't say much on the flight back from Moscow to New York. She slept most of the way and dreamt she was in college working on her thesis about the Royal Danish Egg.

In her dream, she was with Barry and he blabbered on about some movie he had just seen, allowing his nerd side to get the better of him while she did research for her paper. Barry continued to go on and on about some action scene that he thought was the most amazing thing he'd ever seen filmed. It was when he did his impressions of the explosions that the dream blended with her reality and became a nightmare in the sky.

The dream flashed from Becca working on her thesis to her puzzle pieces of information about the Royal Danish Egg, to the airport battle, and seeing Edward beating Vivian. She dreamt the helicopter had crashed, then slid toward her and she couldn't move.

She heard Ed's voice as the helicopter rolled closer and closer to her. "You're nothing, and you will die as nothing." The propeller came right at her and Becca jolted awake in her seat on the plane.

She looked around the private plane and everything that had happened returned to her instantly. She rubbed her face with her hands and stretched her arms.

RC sat across from some Griffin members and he looked to be planning something that she couldn't fully understand. Honestly, after everything she had been through, she didn't want to understand what he was currently up to. Winston came up from behind her.

"Ah. Miss Lake, you've awakened. I trust you had a decent rest."

"It was...okay," she lied. "How long was I out?"

"About eight hours."

He was incredibly calm about everything and it unsettled her. Becca leaned forward and winced, immediately grabbing her side. She had forgotten her injured ribs and felt the massive bandage wrapped around her rib cage.

"Not so fast," Winston said. "Remember, you have two cracked ribs on your left side. Also, you're supposed to take it slowly until we reach our destination. I shall inform your mother you've awakened. She will be able to help you bathe and re-bandage before landing. I've taken the liberty to have fresh clothes prepared for you. Would you care for some breakfast?"

It was all in a day's work for Winston. Becca wondered if anything would ever shake his professionalism. "Yes, please, Winston."

"What would you like?" he asked, almost like a proud father, knowing what she had recently been through. "I can make anything you want."

"Chocolate chip pancakes and some scrambled eggs with orange juice, please." Nothing had ever sounded so good to her. It was so basic and she didn't care.

"Right away." Winston smiled and went to make her breakfast.

Vivian came over and helped Becca out of the chair. "I'll take you to the shower."

"There's a shower on this plane?" When Winston had said bathe, she thought he meant when they landed.

"All of the Griffin's planes have showers." Her mother smiled. "Come with me, gently now."

The past few hours were a blur for Becca. She realized she was still in a state of shock from everything, and she didn't pay much attention when they landed at the airport and were escorted out to a small motorcade of cars. She was back in New York City, back on the island where people were so focused on their daily lives, they paid no attention to who you were as you walked by. Becca, RC, and Vivian all sat in the same car.

Becca looked out the window and saw masses of people. She wondered who was a member of the League of Griffins and who was a member of the Brotherhood of the Fox. She didn't feel safe anymore. No one was who he or she appeared to be. Her warning signs were up. She didn't know whom to trust, and she didn't know what the coming days were going to be like.

Becca turned on the TV in the limo and watched the news. A woman was reporting on the helicopter crash in Russia. The same one that Becca had barely survived. The tape scrolling underneath the picture read, Famous Treasure Hunter Edward Lake Dies In Helicopter Crash After Engine Failure. She turned up the sound.

"It is believed that Edward Lake was not on a specific assignment, he was just on vacation," the reporter said.

Becca turned off the TV. The cover story had worked. The world loses another famous person, never knowing the truth. Vacation. It was so simple that no one in the normal world would care. Becca wanted to puke.

"Did we put out that story or the Brotherhood?" Becca asked her mother.

"The Brotherhood," she said.

It impressed Becca how simple the deception was. It was in plain sight and no one would ever know.

"What is the news media saying about the Secret Tower imploding? Did they blame it on the Americans?" Becca asked.

"No. They said the tower crumbled from a construction issue and luckily no one was hurt," Vivian explained.

"But that's not true. A loyal Griffin was killed."

"Becca," RC said. "His body was recovered before the Russians went through the rubble. No one knows we were ever there."

The car arrived outside an old antique shop and RC got out first to make sure it was safe. Then he allowed Vivian and Becca to enter the building. They went into the back room.

Becca noticed symbols of Griffins throughout the shop and knew this was a safe place as well as a real antique shop. In the back room, Mason Carter stood with a few Griffin scientists.

"Rebecca, Vivian. Welcome back to the city," Mason said. "I trust you enjoyed your flight."

"What's all this?" Becca asked, not answering Mason's question. She watched RC close the door behind them.

"Your authentication," RC answered as he handed the Royal Danish Egg to one of the scientists. They quickly got to work examining the egg. "Even though we had done a digital authentication in Russia, this is the physical one. The one that verifies the other tests."

"We found the leak of your possible relation to the bloodline of Anastasia," Mason explained. "It was the chef in our Moscow hotel when you presented the egg to us and had DIANA do the scan. He thought he'd make a few bucks selling secrets, not to our enemies, but to the world. The money trail was easy to track and he now works somewhere no one will believe his claims." Mason looked at Vivian and Becca sincerely. "I'm sorry for the trouble my organization has caused you both."

"I needed a change of lifestyle anyway, sir," Vivian replied.

"Today we will find out how much of a change that will be. Please take your seats," Mason said.

Becca slowly sat down in a chair next to Vivian, winced, then looked at RC, worried. He sent her a reassuring look that everything would be fine.

They watched the scientists work on the authentication process.

One took out the picture and scanned it while the other dealt with the egg.

"We found a fingerprint on the photo, Mr. Carter," one of the technicians said.

"Run it," Mason replied.

They uploaded the print to DIANA and ran it through a fingerprint database.

"I have all my people at the news outlets currently stalling on the breaking news story," Mason said. "Speaking frankly, this won't be controlled for very long, as it has already spread like wildfire across the Internet. We've bought ourselves some time letting the world think you both are in the air right now on the way to prove your ancestry. We've digitally removed you and RC from any satellite footage in Moscow. According to the world, you were never there."

"I'm guessing that's not the first time you've had to alter footage," Becca said while looking at RC.

"Wouldn't you like to know," he responded with a wink.

"No, Rebecca. I've had to remove RC from many digital forms of media. Too many, in fact." She could tell Mason hadn't approved of RC's ways.

"Sir," one of the scientists interrupted. He'd been working on authenticating the Royal Danish Egg. "This is indeed the lost Royal Danish Egg designed by Peter Carl Fabergé. Shall I have it sent to restoration?"

"Not yet. I'll have Winston take care of it." The scientist nodded.

"So what happens now?" Becca asked Mason.

"Give it a few more minutes, then I'll be able to officially tell you the best course of action," he replied.

"So much for going to college like a normal person, now that the story is everywhere," Becca said.

"This will blow over in a few weeks or so. Another news headline will replace this one." Vivian answered. "Not many people nowadays know or care about the Romanovs. It's ancient history.

Those who know their story will be interested for a minute, then go on with their lives. If you're uncomfortable with any undue interest, you can have a tutor or get your degree online. It's the Brotherhood that we'll always have to worry about. They'll respond to this somehow and it won't be pretty."

The machines beeped. Becca didn't even look at the results.

"How's it looking?" Mason asked the scientists.

"According to DNA from the picture and the cheek swabs from Rebecca and Vivian Lake, they are both a 96% match, exactly as DIANA had predicted."

"Will I be getting a new assignment?" RC asked his dad.

"Your assignment, RC, is to stay close and watch over them until I have had time to organize a formal announcement to the world," Mason said.

Becca could tell RC did want a new assignment, but he was okay with being temporarily assigned as protector to Becca and Vivian, even though Vivian could take care of herself.

Becca turned to Mason. "Do I still have time to see my favorite parts of the city before the announcement?" she asked Mason.

The look on Mason's face said he didn't approve but instead he pointed to RC and said, "He goes with you."

Becca agreed to the terms.

"I'm going to get some R&R," Vivian said. She faced Mason. "Will you have someone clear out my apartment and handle all the paperwork?"

"Being done as we speak," Mason said.

"Thank you. I will report in later this evening." Vivian got up from the chair with a slight groan and gave Becca a big hug. "Be safe. Please."

"I will," Becca replied. "I just have a best friend I need to see."

"Tell Barry I said hello." Vivian smiled and went for the door.

"Oh, Becca," Mason began. "I will need you to report to HQ tonight at eight o'clock sharp. RC will escort you." The way he said it with such authority, Becca knew she had no choice but to nod, acknowledging she would be present. It was shocking how she felt no urge to protest when it came to Mason's demands.

She walked over to RC, who opened the door for her and followed her out onto the streets of New York.

28

"Oh my God," Barry said. "Becca, are you okay?" He referred to her recent adventure in Moscow and the fiasco with her father.

"I don't know if I ever will be," Becca said, being perfectly honest with him and herself. It was nice to be chatting with Barry again face-to-face in a small coffee shop in New York. She felt like herself for a few moments until she saw RC watching them from a distance, being very bodyguard-like.

"I'm glad you're okay, but I was worried sick," Barry said as he fiddled with the spoon on his table. "Don't get me wrong. I enjoyed learning some of those hacking secrets and learning a little bit more about how the world works, but I hated not knowing if you survived the battle zone. That wasn't cool."

"I know. I'm so sorry, Barry." Becca knew he worried about her and she felt guilty for keeping secrets from him. She didn't like it when her mom did the same thing. Granted, Barry had a much better reason to be worried considering he knew that the last time he spoke with her a battle was about to happen. "It was for your own good, and honestly, I didn't know what was happening most of the time."

She watched Barry look over at RC who sat at a table near the front door. His leg jittered like when he was at his computer researching. "So, are you and Mr. GQ a thing now?"

Becca blushed, which made her all the more awkward. "No! God no. It's a little more complicated than that."

Barry saw right through Becca's silence. "Holy mother of God. It's…" Barry quieted and looked around, hoping not to catch anyone's attention. "It's true? I mean you really are related to that Russian family?"

Becca bit her lip.

"Well, you can buy me another coffee then," Barry said.

Barry and Becca shared the biggest laugh. It felt so good to laugh again with him. She had almost forgotten how it felt. Tears came to her eyes as the laughter became almost uncontrollable. She even saw RC watching them and knew he didn't understand why they were laughing so hard, which started the laughter all over again.

"I missed you, Becca," Barry said. He sounded wistful. Lost.

"I missed you too," Becca said as she slowly gained control of herself.

Barry leaned forward and spoke quietly "So what happens now with your life?"

"I don't know and I'm not sure I want to know." Becca took another sip of her coffee. "I haven't really wrapped my head around it."

"Oh, come on. You'll have servants. Plenty of dogs." Barry attempted to cheer her up.

"I'm not Queen Elizabeth, Barry. Although Corgis are very cute."

Barry shifted in his seat. "You seem the same to me."

"How are your parents?" Becca asked to change the subject. "I haven't seen them in a while."

Barry hesitated. His hands shook a little. "They're…fine. They've been a royal pain in the ass recently. I really can't say anything compared to what you've been through, though." He did have a point.

Becca wanted to trade lifestyles with Barry to maintain

normalcy. Every moment that passed felt as if she had lost more and more of her previous life. Her innocence. She had changed. She knew it and she wasn't ready for it, or the responsibility of what was required.

"Where is the egg now?" Barry asked.

"I don't know. It was authenticated and going to be refurbished. It's probably the last time I'll ever see it. It's all so strange, Barry. The secrecy. Pretending like nothing happened. I don't know if I can do it."

Barry fidgeted in his seat again. "Are they going to release it to a museum or put it in a Fabergé exhibit?"

"I have no idea." Becca felt the hairs on the back of her neck stand up. "Why are you so interested in the egg now? Are you okay?" She looked at him for a long moment.

"I'm curious." His demeanor changed immediately. "My best..." He cut himself off as the server brought their food to the table and left. "My best friend found it. I think she deserves some sort of reward or compensation, considering." Barry's response didn't seem entirely truthful. He grabbed the ketchup and poured it over his eggs.

"You know, nothing has been mentioned about that. Considering I had a tower practically collapse on me, I think I should get paid something." Becca watched him pour more ketchup on his eggs. More than he usually did. He started spreading it around.

"What are you doing, Barry? You've smothered your eggs." He seemed off, but she didn't know why.

Barry continued to shift and move his eggs around. "These are the best eggs in New York. You've been gone a while. Figured you needed a refresher as to what good food tastes like."

Weird response, Becca thought.

"Want some eggs?" he asked.

"No, thank you. I have plenty of food." Becca looked at the waffle she hadn't touched yet.

"I insist. You won't regret it. Have some."

"No, really, Barry I don't want any..." She froze as she watched Barry turn his plate of scrambled eggs around to show her.

He had drawn the symbol of the Brotherhood of the Fox on his eggs and wrote on top of it with the ketchup. RUN.

She looked up to Barry, her best friend in the world, and felt her heartbreak. Tears formed in her eyes.

"Barry?" She finally saw him and all that had been troubling him, making him fidget in his seat. How could she be so stupid? He had been acting strange from the moment she'd arrived at the coffee house. She honestly thought it was because of her ancestry and that he had worried about her overseas. She never saw this coming.

"You're missing out on all the fun." He quickly scooped up a bite of eggs and ate it to mess up the fox design on his plate in case he was being watched, which he probably was.

"Okay, you're right." He spoke with his mouth full. "Too much ketchup." He grabbed his coffee and finished what was left. He looked around for the server and Becca saw an earpiece in his right ear. It dawned on her that he was trying to tell her from the moment she got there to get away from him.

Her eyes met his and she saw the panic and the fear that she had grown accustomed to herself. He scooped up some more eggs and purposefully missed his mouth, causing the eggs to fall on his jacket.

"Oh, damn it." He grabbed a napkin, wiped the eggs off, and partially unzipped his jacket revealing a vest with wires underneath. In that moment she knew he wasn't a member of the Brotherhood. He was a pawn, trapped and currently being used by the Brotherhood. Her worst fear, everything RC had warned Becca about from the beginning, had come true.

Becca forced herself to focus. "Where did your parents go on vacation again?" she asked with an alternate meaning, knowing that she and Barry were finally on the same page. She saw Barry's eyes tear up.

"Ugh. Mount Otemanu. It's in Bora Bora. Really far away from here," Barry said as a tear fell down his cheek.

She knew the only true statement in that sentence was, really far away from here. Most likely meaning the worst. His parents were dead.

She did her best to not let her emotions show, however her stomach was in knots for Barry. His parents had been very kind people, and they didn't have much money. They'd never go to Bora Bora unless they'd won the lottery. She knew that for a fact.

"I want to look it up." Becca casually went on her phone and texted RC. *Bomb. Barry trapped.* "It looks beautiful," Becca said, referring to the fake conversation they were having.

"I'm going to visit them after this," Barry said.

Becca looked up from her phone to meet Barry's eyes, knowing what he meant. Tears formed in her eyes. "But I just got back. Surely you can stay longer." She placed her hand on Barry's. If Barry had one look in his eyes, it was I'm sorry. She didn't blame him. She blamed herself for putting him in this danger. "You're my best friend in the entire world."

She looked at RC and saw him get the text. He immediately looked up and made a frantic call on his phone. She couldn't understand what he said. She returned her attention to Barry. "Give your family my love," Becca said trying not to let the tears fall. Her phone beeped and it was a text from RC. *Coffee Bar!*

"Bring them down, Becca," Barry said, letting his tears fall.

Becca ran for the coffee bar and dove behind it.

BOOM!

The windows to the coffee shop blew out, tables and chairs splintered and flew through the air, food went everywhere, shelves were knocked down, and dust, smoke, and debris filled the air.

New Yorkers ran from the area in a panic. Some stayed across the street looking at the damage. RC ran into the destruction.

"Becca! BECCA!" He searched through the debris and helped a patron up. It wasn't Becca. "BECCA!"

"I'm here," she coughed from behind the bar. He came over to her and helped her up. She was okay, only cuts and bruises. She held on to him, hugging him tighter than she'd ever hugged him before.

"They got him," she cried. "They got Barry! He didn't do anything wrong." She cried her heart out. All she could do was repeat the question in her mind. *"WHY?"* she yelled at RC. "Why? Why? Why?"

"Come on," he said. "We have to get out of here. Now." RC helped Becca slip out the back, away from the public eye.

29

Becca sat on the bed in a very fancy bedroom in the Carters' household, not moving, just crying her eyes out to her mother. "He didn't deserve that," she said in between bawling tears. "Why couldn't they have left him alone?"

"It's what they do, sweetheart. That's how the Brotherhood of the Fox operates," Vivian said.

"I hate them!" Becca said. "I hate them!" She felt rage in her heart, more so from the loss of Barry than Edward. When she had flown back from Russia, it bothered her that she hadn't shed a single tear for stopping Edward Lake and crossing a line she never thought she'd ever cross.

She wondered if she was a monster for not having a shred of emotion for killing the man who had abused her mother and been disgusted by her very own existence. It was an entirely different story when it came to Barry, the only non-blood relative who had always been there for her, through better and through worse. He was the only one she had trusted her entire life. She missed him so much, and wished she could change the past. She wished she could erase the last images of him begging for her to help him in his final moments.

"It's all my fault. If I had never started writing that stupid thesis, and never found the egg, Barry would still be alive and safe."

"There was no way you could have known." Vivian tried to comfort Becca.

"I was so blind," Becca said.

"No, you weren't. You were distracted," RC said as he entered the room in nicer clothes than he usually wore. "Anyone would have missed the signs Barry gave off when you were too busy trying to survive yourself. I'm sorry for your loss, and I'm sorry I didn't see it coming either."

Becca didn't know how to stop blaming herself. What was done was done. She had messed up, and paid dearly for it.

"I don't know what to do now," Becca said.

"Follow me, please," RC said.

"What? Where are we going?" She looked at her mother, who nodded for her to go with him. Becca didn't want to go anywhere but she had no energy left to protest. She followed RC out of the bedroom, through the massively beautiful maze of the Carter mansion. She didn't care about all the priceless pieces of art that hung on the hallway walls, the beautiful statues made of marble and bronze. All she thought about was the pain in her heart and how to make it stop. She didn't know a person could feel so hurt and so enraged at the same time.

RC brought Becca and Vivian to an elevator. Normally, she would have been impressed, but everything had changed. She just decided to go with it. Who cared about an elevator in a house anyway? The elevator went down what would have been several floors before stopping.

The Carter mansion wasn't just a mansion. It was a fortress. The elevator doors opened to a beautifully decorated stone hallway with a red carpet and massive pillars. No doubt, the pillars were part of the foundation for the Carters' home.

"What is this?" Becca asked.

"The League of Griffins headquarters in New York," RC

explained as they walked down the hallway. "Try not to touch anything. This place is hundreds of years old."

As they walked down the long hallway, Becca looked at old paintings in the style of Rembrandt and other famous painters, depicting different people with the symbol of a Griffin painted behind them. It was like being in a medieval museum. She saw there was a small library to her right.

"That is where you will learn the history of our forefathers and mothers who helped the Griffins survive for as long as we have. You will learn about artifacts we retrieved, the operations required to do so, the squads involved, and the cover-ups released to the public."

They continued to another room where Becca saw men and women around her age and older sparring with each other and training in agility, weapons, and close-quarters combat. "That's where you learn to become a badass." RC pointed to the training grounds.

It looked intense to Becca, like Crossfit for superheroes. She did see a few obstacles and challenges she wanted to learn how to do. She watched a woman, who had to be in her early twenties, go from a standing position next to a wall and with one step climb up the wall to the top. That impressed her.

"You trained here?" Becca asked her mother.

"All the time. It's my home," Vivian said as they turned a corner and entered a two-story oval room with gorgeous Griffin décor. RC stopped and faced Becca.

"Please enter the center of the circle," he said.

She looked at him, worried.

"It's okay, trust me," he said in a less formal way.

Becca stepped cautiously into the middle of the circle and stood still, looking around. Her mother stayed behind with RC.

"Rebecca Hunter Lake." Mason's voice echoed throughout the room.

Becca looked up and saw Mason dressed in a ceremonial robe

and more people dressed in the same robes, wearing hoods. They circled around Becca.

"At the young age of eighteen you have proven yourself to be trustworthy," Mason began, "incredibly intelligent, and a true protector of mankind. You have risked your life for family and friends and made sacrifices no one should have to endure. You have the fire of a true Griffin burning within you and we welcome you to the nest. You upheld the tenets of the League of Griffins. "Honesty, loyalty and secrecy at all costs!"

"Honesty, loyalty and secrecy at all costs!" everyone in the room repeated. The power of the words and the strength behind them sent chills up Becca's spine. She looked at her mother and saw an incredibly proud look on her face. She saw love in her smile mixed with relief that she didn't have to keep this part of her life a secret from her anymore.

"Now I ask you this," Mason continued, "Do you want to serve mankind from the shadows of secrecy? Protect the world from the Brotherhood of the Fox?"

She looked up at Mason, who stood on a small balcony surrounded by four more members of the League of Griffins. They had to be the head honchos who helped Mason run this organization.

"I want to destroy the Brotherhood of the Fox." She stared unblinking into Mason's eyes. She stood her ground and allowed herself to feel the rage burning inside her.

She caught movement from other Griffins out of the corner of her eye. Clearly, that wasn't something they were expecting her to say. She saw Mason smile at her response in approval and understanding.

"Rebecca Hunter Lake, you have earned the rank of The Order of the Wing for enduring hazardous conditions while searching out invaluable information for the League of Griffins. Please step forward and hold out your right wrist."

She did as told, and her mother walked up to her. She had what appeared to be a handheld needleless tattoo machine.

"You'll feel a bit of a sting," Vivian said. A blue light projected onto the underside of her right wrist with the outline of a Griffin's wing. She saw a laser brand the wing symbol onto her wrist. She winced at the branding, more from being startled than pain. It was over in two seconds. There, on the right side of her wrist was a flesh-colored brand that you'd miss if you didn't look for it. She looked up at her mother and recognized the same fire in her eyes. Vivian smiled the proudest smile Becca thought she had ever seen from her mother.

"Welcome to the League of Griffins."

THE LEAGUE OF GRIFFINS TATTOOS

Griffin beak-Leader of the organization
Griffin claw-Attack squad
Griffin talons-Assassins
Griffin wings-Information gatherers
Griffin feather-Trusted advisors

ABOUT THE AUTHOR

Barb Goodwin was a flight attendant before she turned to writing. The Lost Treasures series is about famous, still missing treasures. Barb has two sisters, one an identical twin, and they are all best friends. Her wonderful nephew is her co-author for the Lost Treasures series and he always brings laughter to their writing sessions.

ABOUT THE AUTHOR

Doug Penikas is an actor, dancer, and filmmaker. He has performed in numerous films and television shows for many years, as well as music videos, and live musicals. He is passionate about storytelling in all forms and is thrilled to be a co-author with his aunt Barb Goodwin on the Lost Treasures series. Doug lives in California.

Made in the USA
Las Vegas, NV
27 June 2023

73972721R00111